SUICIDE WOODS

Suicide Woods

STORIES

..

Benjamin Percy

Graywolf Press

This publication is made possible, in part, by the voters of Minnesota through a Minnesota State Arts Board Operating Support grant, thanks to a legislative appropriation from the arts and cultural heritage fund. Significant support has also been provided by Target, the McKnight Foundation, the Lannan Foundation, the Amazon Literary Partnership, and other generous contributions from foundations, corporations, and individuals. To these organizations and individuals we offer our heartfelt thanks.

MINNESOTA
STATE ARTS BOARD

CLEAN
WATER
LAND &
LEGACY
AMENDMENT

TARGET.

Published by Graywolf Press
250 Third Avenue North, Suite 600
Minneapolis, Minnesota 55401

All rights reserved.

www.graywolfpress.org

Published in the United States of America

ISBN 978-1-64445-006-2

2 4 6 8 9 7 5 3 1
First Graywolf Printing, 2019

Library of Congress Control Number: 2019931353

Cover design: Kyle G. Hunter

Cover art: © Anirut Kongsorn / Getty Images

For Lisa

Contents

SUICIDE WOODS

The Cold Boy

The forest is hardwood, and the branches of the oaks and sycamores are bare except for the crows, hundreds of them, all huddled like little men in black jackets. Together they make a strange music—muttering to one another in rusty voices as they click their beaks and rustle their feathers and claw at the bark—that can be heard a quarter mile away, across a snowy cornfield, where Ray stands on a frozen pond.

The stubs of last year's cornstalks fang through the snow, and two sets of footprints lead like a rough blue stream from his house to the pond. Two sets of footprints, yet he is alone on the ice. The cold rises through the soles of his boots, creeping up his legs, into his chest, so that his heart feels frosted with tiny white crystals.

The pond is big, close to two acres, with three holes melted into its ice from the warm springs beneath. The holes are big enough to drive a car through, the ice at their rims gradually thinning into a gray sliver that gives way to the dark water at their centers.

His house, a ranch with a black roof and tan siding, sits fifty yards away. Next to it, a red pole barn, where he stores his johnboat and runs his taxidermy business. From where Ray stands, he

can see his shop window, a square cut into the corrugated metal—
and from there, he could have seen his nephew leave the house
and crunch through the calf-deep snow, heading toward the pond,
probably with his arms held out like wings to keep his balance. Had
Ray only looked up from his work—a rack-mount job, a deer shot by
Jacob Henderson—there would have been time to lift the window
and yell, to scramble out the side door and through the snow and
grab the boy by the coat and give him a shake and say, What the
hell are you doing? Had he only looked up, he wouldn't be standing here now, where the footprints concluded, at the edge of a hole
as black and reflective as the glass eye he'd nudged into the deer's
empty socket minutes ago.

The boy was supposed to be watching cartoons. The boy, seven
years old—or was it six?—with his fair skin, his hair so blond it is
nearly white. Ray hardly knows him, sees him only on holidays and
when his sister drives down from Saint Paul to visit. The boy rarely
speaks, and when he does, his voice comes out in a high whisper.
His eyes are the blue-black color of the dirty snow piled at the edges
of the highway.

And now the boy is trapped beneath the ice, his tiny body floating there, turning around and around in what must look like a cave
with three columns of light streaming from the holes punched in
its roof.

Ray doesn't know what to do. Call his sister or call the police.
There is no rush—the boy is dead, has to be—but Ray feels a horrible need to act, even if that means stepping forward, as if through
a trapdoor, allowing the cold water to squeeze the breath from him.
It would be better than facing his sister, the hate he imagines twisting her face.

In this moment—on the pond, in the middle of the snow-
scalloped cornfield—Ray feels mixed-up with anger and regret
and sadness. Every stupid protest cycles through his head: "I wish
I could trade places with the boy," "I wish I could turn back time,"
and so on.

Then, as if summoned, the boy's body appears below him. One moment water sucks and plops at the edges of the hole—and the next, the boy is there, his face a white smear rising out of the darkness.

At first Ray does nothing, dazed and blinking. Even when he wants to move, a second later, his joints feel rusted and his boots rooted to the ice. How long has he been standing here—ten minutes, twenty? He staggers forward, and the ice moans, and cracks spread beneath him, thin black creeks that threaten to open up and swallow him. He gets down on his knees, slowly, out of stiffness and caution, and then goes flat, bellies up to the ice to distribute his weight.

He can't see from this angle, his cheek resting against the ice. He slides forward and reaches out blindly for the hole, his fingers splashing at the edge of it. The slushy perimeter crumbles, and his arm drops into the water up to his elbow. His curse is cut short when he feels something catch hold of him. At first he thinks some starved fish has risen from the depths to bite at his fingers, mistaking them for nightcrawlers. But when he yanks back his arm, he feels the tug of weight and sees the small white hand clamped onto his.

Later, he will wonder at the impossibility. He will remember stories from Sunday school and late-night television about miracles, about cold-water survival. He will read on the Internet about the girl from Utah who fell through the ice when skating and survived after more than an hour underwater. And about the man in Indiana who spiraled his Jeep off a bridge and into a frozen river, trapped below for thirty minutes. "There has never been a drug more effective or mysterious than the cold," reads a quote from a doctor. Ray will read about cryogenics, about Walt Disney's head preserved in a deep-freeze storage locker somewhere, awaiting resurrection. He will think of everything, and then nothing, concentrating only on the relief he feels.

Because it is impossible to think. He acts—pure reflex. Crying out to the boy, telling him, "Hold on! I've got you!" Ray scrabbles backward, drawing the body from the water, some of the ice giving way, the hole opening wider as if reluctant to give up its quarry. The boy is laid out on his back. He wears a red jacket, blue jeans, black boots, all of them bleeding water. Ray picks him up and strangles him into a hug. The day is so cold that the pondwater on his skin freezes almost instantly, a glassy sheath. Ray tries roughly to rub some warmth into the boy, and against his hand the ice cracks and falls away in shards.

The boy's eyes are open, but he is not breathing. Ray imagines the water inside him hardening into spikes that stab through his lungs. He doesn't really know what he's doing, but he's seen enough movies and television shows to make a go of it, when he sets the boy down and presses his chest—once, twice, three times—and then brings their mouths together and breathes into the boy and thinks, "Please, please." After three minutes of this, of Ray alternately pounding and blowing and calling down favors from a god he doesn't believe in, the boy convulses and gags. Ray turns him on his side so that he can more easily cough out the pinkish water mixed up with bile, the remnants of the bowl of Froot Loops he ate that morning in front of the television.

"Are you all right?" Ray says.

The boy sits up and rubs his eye and looks at Ray and Ray looks at the boy and neither of them says anything.

A county highway runs along the edge of the cornfield, and beyond it rises the forest. An old Chevy pickup comes rattling along, and when it stutters in its progress, and backfires, the crows cackle madly and take to the air and leave the trees as naked as skeletons.

Two weeks earlier his sister, Helen, had called him to beg a favor. Some man—there was always some man, Ray couldn't keep track of them all—wanted to take her on a cruise. "The Bahamas," she said. "At this time of year. My God! And he's paying for everything. All you can eat, all you can drink. I really, really want to do this," she said.

"So do it."

"That's the thing." She needed him to watch the boy. "I'd owe you big-time. I'd even pay you."

Ray said he wasn't sure. This was a busy time of year, his storage locker full of trophies from hunting season. Plus, he hardly knew the boy. What would they talk about? What would they do? And Helen said, "That's exactly why this would be so great." This would be his chance to get to know him, to be a good uncle.

"You'll be fine," she said. "He's no trouble."

In the living room, he lays the boy down and strips off his jacket, his clothes, tosses them aside in a sodden pile that darkens the carpet. Ray is hopped-up on adrenaline that chatters his teeth and sends shivers through his body, but the boy is as still as a sculpture. Even when stripped naked, he remains silent and motionless, his skin white, blue around the edges, like some icewater mollusk scraped from its shell. Ray wraps him in heavy blankets. A smell comes off him—the smell of the pond, of mud and algae and fish.

Ray says, "Shit, shit, shit" under his breath when he charges through the house. He cranks the thermostat to eighty. He starts a hot bath. He peels off the lid of a can of beef stew and slops it in a bowl to throw in the microwave.

When he returns to the living room, the boy has shrugged off the blankets. He is watching cartoons with his legs folded beneath his knees, the watery light of the television playing across his body.

Ray thinks about taking the boy to the hospital. But then he imagines all the problems that will follow. His sister works as a secretary—no, that isn't the term she uses, administrative assistant—at the auto parts dealer, and she regularly grouses about her insurance: the copays, the sky-high deductibles, the denied coverage. He would have to call her to get her policy info. She left him an emergency contact number for the cruise ship. He isn't so much concerned about ruining her trip as he is about getting an earful after she learns what happened. The doctors would no doubt run tests, would keep the boy overnight for observation, and in the end Ray knows he would foot the bill. He wonders if the police would get involved. Maybe it was neglectful, even illegal, for him to have left the boy alone. How should he know? And then there would be the reporters. He imagines them gathering at the end of his driveway, their cameras like shotguns trained at his house, the pond—all of them eager to tell the story of the miracle boy and his deadbeat uncle.

There's no reason to make a lot of trouble out of nothing, not when everything is fine. The boy is fine.

Except that Ray can't seem to warm him up, his skin the color and feel of sunlit snow. The few times that Ray touches the boy, leading him from the television to the kitchen table, from the bathroom to the guest room, he startles at the cold, clammy skin and yanks back his hand.

Nor will the boy eat. Ray tries soups, hot cocoa, grilled cheese sandwiches oozing with Velveeta. The boy takes the occasional sip or nibble, but otherwise he simply stares at the food, not saying anything, even when Ray throws up his hands and says, "Well, what do you want, then? You've got to eat something."

Later, he catches the boy in the kitchen. The freezer door is open and the cold is blasting from it and the boy is scooping chocolate ripple ice cream from the carton into his mouth. Ray lets the boy eat as much as he wants, and the boy wants it all. He chews the ice cream, big spoonfuls of it, his mouth a smacking mess. When his spoon scrapes the bottom of the carton, the boy drops the carton to the floor, where it blurps out a tongue of chocolate on the linoleum. The boy looks to Ray expectantly, and Ray stutters out a few apologies, says he doesn't have any more ice cream, says they can pick some up at the Fareway later. Then he gets an idea and says he'll be right back and pulls a bowl from the cupboard and throws on a coat and heads outside.

A gasp of cold greets him. The wind has shaped the snow into drifts, like the sluggish waves of some frozen ocean. The day is sunny, but the yard is dark and rippling with shadows, and Ray feels momentarily unbalanced as he staggers off the front step. The crows are overhead, hundreds of them, a circling black eddy that blots out the sun.

He keeps an eye on them—as if at any moment they might descend and carry him off—when he kneels to fill the bowl with snow. It is only minutes later, after he pours maple syrup over the snow and sets the treat on the kitchen table, after the boy begins to carve his spoon into it, that Ray notices a bit of black mixed up in all that white. A feather. He grabs the boy by the wrist, stops the spoon inches from his open mouth. Slowly the boy turns his head to stare at Ray and tightens face into a hateful expression, hissing.

Ray wakes shivering in the night. The window next to his bed is open. The wind moans through it, and the curtains breathe inward, green and trembling like seaweed. He jumps out of bed and slams shut the window. The curtains settle, but the moaning only shifts to another part of the house. He grabs a sweatshirt from the dirty laundry in the corner and pulls it on when he staggers into the hallway, where the wind blows and the carpet fibers feel like frozen blades of grass.

He finds every window in the house open, an invitation to the severe wind that flutters newspaper pages across his living room, that ruffles the bear pelt hanging from the wall, that knocks over a plastic gas station cup and freezes the milk in a half-eaten bowl of cereal. He rushes to close them all, to stop the wind from coming in, while also chasing the sense that something might escape him, the boy.

There are two bedrooms in the house—one belongs to him and the other to a futon and a garage-sale bench press and a wobbly desk, on top of which perches an old IBM computer in a nest of receipts. He finds the boy asleep on the futon. He has kicked off his covers and lies there with his legs and arms splayed, as if he is floating.

When Ray closes this final window, a hush falls over the house. He can hear the rasp of the boy's breath—and something else—a faint cackling from outside. The window is already steaming over, and he wipes a hand through the condensation to reveal the moon, a full yellow moon darkened by what appears to be a cloud scudding across it. But the cloud moves too fast. And when Ray looks closer he sees the cloud for what it is, a seething mass of crows.

In the morning the boy's sheets are wet. A damp oval in the shape of him. It does not smell like urine or sweat. It smells like pondwater.

Ray is stripping the sheets off the futon when the phone rings. He goes to the kitchen and for a long time stares at it—the black snail of a unit hanging next to the fridge—before picking it up.

"Why did you take so long to answer?" his sister says.

"I was busy."

He imagines her bringing her hand to her heart, like she always does, when she says, "I thought something was wrong."

No, nothing is wrong. Nothing at all.

"Are you two getting along?"

Yes.

"That's good. That's what I want to hear. You know why? Because I feel happy as shit right now, and I'm not looking to spoil that feeling." The cruise is amazing. The food is amazing. She has an amazing tan. She has made amazing friends. While they are in Nassau, she is going to get her hair braided and then maybe go parasailing and play some blackjack at the casino.

Ray thinks he can hear calypso music in the background, a steel drum. He fades out the buzz of her voice, startling when she yells, "I said, what's my boy up to?"

The phone feels like a brick pressed against his ear. He is watching the boy, and the boy is watching cartoons, is turning his head to observe Ray with eyes that look more black than blue.

"Watching some TV."

"Don't bother him, then. Tell him I love him, the little shit." She laughs her throaty laugh, and Ray imagines a cloud of cigarette smoke. "Tell him I'll see him soon enough."

"I'll tell him that. I will."

The walls of the house are pine paneled and studded with dead animals. A twelve-point buck, its antlers a thorned basket. Three quail suspended in flight. An opossum clambering up a log and showing its needled teeth. A bobcat pawing playfully at a largemouth bass. The skin of a black bear, its legs splayed in an X, so that it appears to have been hurled and flattened against the wall.

The smell of formaldehyde hangs like an ammonia cloud in the house and in the pole barn, and it puffs off his clothes, his hands and hair. He doesn't notice it, but others do. His buddies say he smells like he rolled around in a funeral parlor. When his sister visits—with her big hair and her long purple fingernails—she waves a hand in front of her face and says, "Pee-you." And when he sometimes goes out to dinner at Dangerous Curves, a gentlemen's club with a buffet supper, the women will dance for him, will smile and snake around him, but when they lean close, their powdered breasts brushing against his cheeks, he notices how their noses crinkle, some of them asking about his cologne.

Ray orders his parts—his claws and jawsets and tongues and tails, his flex eyes and pinpoints and standard pupils, his polyurethane forms for deer—from an online store that delivers via UPS a few times a month. But his chemicals come from a specialty company based out of Rochester. Dyes and resins. Adhesives and sealants and preservatives. A few times a year he drives there and back, the bed of his pickup sloshing with the buckets and bottles he buys in bulk. This morning, the morning after the boy fell in the pond, he peels open a bucket of formaldehyde, and the fumes that boil out of it make him weep. He will wipe at his face, wipe away with the heels of his hands the tears wetting his cheeks. This is the only time he cries. Not when his father died of a stroke. Not when he sent his mother to the nursing home after she lost her mind and ability to cook and clean. Not when his girlfriend of ten years—Tanya—said to hell with him if he didn't want kids, didn't want to get married, didn't really want to spend time with her except the occasional buffet dinner followed by a quick and dirty screw. His sister had always called him cold.

He is cold now, in the pole barn, in the walk-in freezer. He is surrounded by shelves of animals, all packaged in plastic, their ID tags scrawled over with a Sharpie that identifies their owner, their date of entry, their order number. He stuffs deer mostly, but also bears, beavers, bobcats, turkeys, pheasant. He makes throw rugs, doeskin gloves, one time a pair of moccasins, though that was a pain in the ass and he would never do it again. He mounts fish on logs and antlers on stained oak and red velvet.

He comes in this morning to work on a dog, a pug owned by Ruth Gill, a square-shaped woman who teaches English at the local community college and always wears floral-patterned muumuus, her hair a frizzy red helmet. The dog was named Nosferatu, and she had euthanized it. "Cancer," she said. "They all die of cancer. It's the dog food that does it." She would dress the dog up in tuxedos, sailor suits, tracksuits. Ray would often see them around town—at the mall, the farmers market—the pug bug-eyed and snorting at the end of a leash. Since dropping off the dog, Ruth has called daily to check in, often sobbing, always wanting to know when Ray will be done, when Nosferatu can come home. "Soon," he tells her and means it, moving the dog up in his processing schedule so that he can put an end to her pestering.

When Ray is in the freezer, pawing through the stacks of bodies, thumbing their tags, searching for the pug, he comes across a crow. It is not packaged, not tagged. Some people have crows for pets. And sometimes the weirdos—the people with the powder-white faces and the black lipstick and the chains running from their lips to their earlobes—sometimes they drop off a carcass to stuff. But he has no idea where this crow came from. It is the size of his forearm, deeply black, its wings neatly folded against its sides. He picks it up, its feathers like brittle blades of obsidian, its beak open and decorated with hoarfrost that looks like lace or mold—and then drops it and wipes his hand on his jeans and locates the pug and carries its body into the shop, to the stainless steel table with the drain beneath it. Here he will skin it and set the fur aside to clean and dry and oil. The remains—a shrunken pod of bone and muscle—he will dip into plaster of Paris to equal the shape of its body. And then he will make a matching fiberglass mold to sew the skin around. Pluck from a shelf some glass eyes, teeth.

But that will come later. For now, the dog—such a hideous dog, some things should be buried and forgotten—must thaw. He plugs in a space heater. In a few minutes, he knows, the dog will appear to move, to breathe, as it softens. Gases will escape it. Joints will unspring.

He startles at a noise—a crunching and snapping—behind him. The boy sits on a folding chair, swinging his legs in a scissoring motion. Ray doesn't like the boy's eyes. The way they stare at him, unblinking. He would prefer to lock him in a bedroom or plant him in front of the television. But he knows he must keep him close. Earlier, Ray gave him a glass of Coke. The boy has since sucked it down and now chews on the ice, working the cubes around in his mouth, slowly crushing them with his teeth, making a noise like bones breaking.

Helen will be home soon. In two more days she will fly from Fort Lauderdale to Minneapolis and grumble up the driveway in her Grand Prix and crash through the door without knocking. Where's my baby? she will say, fatter, tanner, grinning widely. Will she even notice any difference? Will the boy smile when he sees her, spring up from his place in front of the television and run into her arms? Will she mess his cheek with lipstick? Will he tell her what happened, how the ice opened up beneath him?

Ray hopes so. At least that would be something—right now the boy seems capable of nothing, seems to belong to another world.

He cries constantly, though not out of pain or sadness, not as far as Ray can tell. It is as though he is leaking. Maybe melting. Spilling over as if some secret spring inside him has been tapped. Tears dribble down his cheeks. The damp impressions of his fingertips can be found throughout the house, on the windows, the kitchen table, the TV remote. And when he walks across the carpet—slowly now, and hunched over, like an old man whose muscles have gone flaccid, whose joints are clotted with rust—he leaves behind footprints, the carpet damp and decorated with half-moon designs.

He won't eat anymore. Not even the open cartons of ice cream that Ray sets in front of him, a spoon thrust into them, Neapolitan, cookie dough, chocolate fudge triple chunk. "Come on," Ray says. "Snap out of it." The boy sleeps most of the day. Curled up on the living room floor or sprawled out on the futon. Ray finds it hard to focus on the boy's face, his features seeming smeared over, as if seen through a rainy window.

There is a cold snap. On television weathermen swing their arms across maps of Minnesota like wizards conjuring winds. Their voices are high-pitched and hurried when they talk about changing pressure systems, plummeting temperatures. They frown when they say, "This is deadly weather, folks. Stay inside." They talk about the bitterness of the air, as if wind had a flavor, the gusts making it feel like forty below. The footage cuts to a shot of a reporter out in a field. He throws a bucket of water into the air, and it transforms into a cloud of crystals. He hammers a nail into a board with a muffin left outside to freeze.

Ray's sister called an hour ago, and he let the machine pick it up. "We're here," she said. "We landed. Waiting for our luggage now. And guess what? We're going to book the next flight back to the Bahamas. Joking! But seriously, why do we live here? The weather is trying to kill us. See you soon! Can't wait to see my sweet boy! Love you!"

Ray looks around the house. At the dead animals nailed to the walls. At the dishes piled up in the sink. At the mail stacked on the table. At the boy sitting in front of the television. He should do something to get ready for her. He picks up an empty ice cream carton off the floor and puts it in a trash can that is already heaped high. He isn't sure when he last took a shower. That's what he should do. A long hot shower and a shave. A fresh shirt. He should try to look like someone you would trust your child with.

Thirty minutes later, he climbs out of the shower and towels off and pulls on his clothes in a bathroom swirling with ghostly steam. A cold current of air streams under the door, and he doesn't think much about it until he turns the knob and steps into the hall, where the wind grips him. His damp hair instantly freezes. He thuds down the hallway and rounds the corner and sees the front door open and swinging. From the walls comes a groaning as the pipes begin to seize up.

He shoves his feet into boots but doesn't have time to find his coat. He runs into the day with an arm held out as if to ward off the cold. The sun shines, its light blurred by the blown snow that swirls all around him. With the lunar quality of winter light and the cratered snowscape of his property, he might as well be on the moon.

Ray cannot see far, visibility reduced to less than fifty yards one minute, ten the next, but he can see enough. A blur of color. The boy still in his pajamas, moving toward pond. Ray tries to run. He lifts his knees high to trudge through the deep snow. Already his fingers and ears, the tip of his nose, have gone numb. A blackness darker than a shadow catches the corner of his eye. He glances down at it. A crow. Dead in the snow. By the time he registers it, he is already upon another, and then another, and another still. Dead crows litter the yard—killed by the cold. At that very moment another appears out of the white oblivion and strikes the ground before him with a thud. His boot crunches over it. More crows fall, one of them crashing painfully against his shoulder, where it will leave a bruise as if its color was contagious.

He can no longer feel his face. His hands are like weights swinging at the ends of his arms. He stumbles onto the pond now, the boy not so far away, ghosting in and out of view. He calls out, "Stop! Stop, dammit!" but the wind carries away his voice. He wonders if the boy will resist him, will lash out with his fingers curled over into bony claws. The thought is interrupted when he spots the hole in the ice and reels backward. Another step, and he would have fallen through.

He spins around in a circle. He is alone. The boy is gone. Swallowed by the pond or erased by the wind. Ray hugs his arms around his chest. His body shudders. His eyes water, the tear trails freezing on his cheeks. The snow is all around him, a white void, and he feels lost and overwhelmed in its changelessness. He knows he will vanish, too, if he doesn't depart this place. He leans into the wind and follows the trail of footprints, the only means by which he can find his way home and the only indication that the boy ever existed. The way is so endlessly cold.

Suspect Zero

5:32 a.m.—November 20—Chippewa County, Wisconsin

People think they know, but they don't. Maybe there was something romantic about a steam engine, but there was nothing romantic about a freight or passenger train. The horn sounded mournful for a reason. There was no place lonelier than an engine car at night. For thirty dollars an hour, sixty hours a week, Mike worked as a conductor, hauling everything but mostly grain, coal, oil. One- or two- or three-engine loads. Flatbeds. Boxcars. Reefers. Hoppers. Cattle cars. Well cars. Wagontops. Hazardous, perishable. It was all the same to him. Stopping every twenty miles, every hundred miles to drop off a load, secure a load, check the air brakes, and then off he went again, alone except for the engineer who snored in a cot and woke only to help him throw switches and uncouple cars, following the tracks, the tracks, the tracks. You see train tracks as fragmented—crossing a rural highway here, cutting through a soybean field there—but Mike understood the through line, the steel stitching that bound everything together. Tracks made most think of faraway places, but to Mike the tracks were a single place that the world scrolled by, unavailable to him.

That was his angle on the world. Separate, watching every-thing and everyone flash by. Sometimes, late at night, he would snap off the lights of the engine car to see more clearly. A shooting star streaked the sky. Teenagers gathered around a bonfire burn-ing in a fallow cornfield. In a window a woman rubbed the back of her colicky baby. So many towns, so many lives, made it somehow harder to care about them all. People mattered less when you saw how many of them there were.

It hurt to blink. It hurt to sit. The doom-doom-doom of the train's progress became his pulse. This night he had gone far enough, long enough, that no matter how much coffee he drank, his eyes crossed, so that one second it appeared the tracks split, and the next, they merged.

That had happened to him once. The tracks had merged in a snarl of metal outside Grand Forks. Some environmentalists pro-testing the North Dakota oil grab had sparked a load of C-4 beneath the tracks. His had been the first train to hit the mess it made. He came around a curve and spotted it. He threw the air brakes, the dynamic brakes, but it wasn't enough. He had a three-man crew, and they leaped from the train and rolled down the gravel berm and watched helplessly when a hundred yards down the line the engine jumped and the rest of the cars accordioned after it. The shriek and boom and clank of warring steel made the air shake and his ears feel as though they might bleed.

That was the only time the tracks connected, when things got mangled.

At a grain elevator near Eau Claire, Wisconsin, the train screeched to a stop, and Mike climbed out to take a piss, walk the load. A so-dium arc lamp buzzed. The green hint of dawn edged the horizon. He snapped on his Maglite to throw a beam, maybe crack a skull. There were always stowaways.

That's what he thought he was dealing with—another stowaway—when he spotted the leg. Jutting from the top of a coal car. A bare foot with a pronounced arch. A delicate ankle that rose into a thin calf. Like someone sleeping, a restless leg peeking out from under the sheets.

He called out, but no one responded. He climbed the ladder and discovered why. The body was already purpling along the edges. No clothes, no identification, no teeth, no hands. No idea where it came from except down the tracks.

..

1:00 a.m.—November 20—Steele County, Minnesota

The red lights flashed their warning, but no bar dropped to block his passage, so Ron considered risking it. At the last second he dropped his foot and the brakes chirped and the truck's grille jerked to a stop a few feet short of the tracks.

The train blasted its horn, whether for him or for the town in the near distance, he didn't know. A deep-bellied, woeful cry. The engine car's one eye—halogen bright—cut through the dark and made Ron turn his head away as if he didn't want to be seen. Then it was past him, and he could feel its progress in his body. The rattle and the chime and the doom-doom-doom as thousands of pounds of steel rolled dangerously forward.

He remembered, as a boy, laying down pennies on the tracks at night, coming back the next morning to find them warped and slivered. One time the tracks were slick as though oiled and he didn't know why until he saw the man cloven in half. Flies buzzed in and out of his open mouth. Ron collected his pennies before walking home to share what he had seen. The paper later said the man was drunk and must have passed out or stumbled and knocked his head. His mother licked her finger when she turned the page to finish the article. "He wasn't himself," she said, looking hard at Ron to impart some lesson. "No one would a done a thing like that on purpose. It's against nature."

A phrase she had used on Ron twice. The first time she said it, when he was ten, he had cut open their cat to see what was inside it. The second time, when he was seventeen, the cops had come for him after a girl in the neighborhood had disappeared. They hadn't been able to prove anything, but his mother knew. She told him she never wanted to see him again. She said he was an abomination. Of course she didn't know what she was talking about. The hens in the coop sometimes ate their own eggs. The neighbor's snake-bit horse raced off a cliff in a panic. The kudzu strangled the trees until they were nothing but gray twigs. Nature was always gobbling itself up.

And then the last car, an oil tank, bulleted by. The red lights stopped flashing. The drumming lingered for a time. He crossed the tracks and followed the county highway as it snaked past stubbled cornfields, leafless woods. He saw no other cars and didn't expect to, not at this hour.

He clicked off his headlights and drove the truck past the two- and three-story homes cut back on forested lots. All of them dark. Everything silvered by the moon hanging low in the sky.

It was still another mile. As though the house was hiding. The asphalt lane terminated at a gravel road that ran off into an orchard. Here he parked, among the bare apple trees, at the edge of a hill that overlooked the train tracks. He killed the ignition. He studied his face in the rearview. The lights from the dash gave him the blue-green pallor of the drowned. He didn't feel excited or nervous or anything really, only the same blank calm someone might experience when pouring milk over cereal or opening a drawer to fetch a pencil. That was the best way to feel in situations like this. Then you didn't make mistakes.

Steam plumed from his mouth when he unfolded himself from the truck. The air tasted of the onset of winter, like an aspirin dissolving on your tongue. He left the door unlocked, the keys on the seat. They would rattle in his pocket, which he had also emptied of coins. He had changed from his work clothes and now wore sneakers, jeans, a hooded sweatshirt, all of them dark colored so that he would appear as a shadow. Except for his gloves, which he pulled on now. Latex. They made his hands glow and appear separate from him.

His footsteps crunched on the gravel and then thudded the blacktop and then scritched the frost-stiffened grass as he returned to the house. He could make himself so quiet when he wanted. His body was slender enough that it sometimes felt like he could cut through the air.

He circled around back. The lawn ended and the stairs began, pea gravel boxed by railroad ties. They led to the deeper darkness behind the house. He took them delicately and slowed at their bottom. The back patio ran up against the walk-out basement. He didn't want to risk tripping over an uneven pavestone, thudding a shin against a planter.

He checked each window—there were four—all of them locked. So he stood by the sliding glass door. There was a reason people so often used a broomstick to buttress these entries; their locks were the easiest to muscle open. He waited for the train. Ninety rolled through each day, so you never had to wait very long between them.

The cold crept into his fingers, and he shook them, flexed them, when the horn finally sounded ten minutes later. The air trembled with the train's passage. The grumble veiled any noise he might make when he took the sliding door's handle in both hands and braced a foot against the frame and leaned back. He strained so hard that his back popped and his veins throbbed and the tendons rose painfully from his neck. Then the casing gave, the lock untoothed from its mooring. The door slid open with a gasp.

..

3:01 p.m.—November 19—Steele County, Minnesota

Laura thought—given the location, more than five miles from town—fewer people would bother her here. But they kept coming. Three visitors in one day. The doorbell would ring—a three-note chime that echoed through the house—and Laura would go still. But whoever was out there, they had to come a long way to visit this house, and that meant they were willing to wait to get inside.

First, the deliveryman hefting a brown box and requesting an electronic signature. Then the Girl Scout hoping to sell Thin Mints for her troop, her bored mother parked in an idling minivan. Then the Mormon boys, in their ties and their short-sleeve, white-collar shirts, who asked for her name and a minute of her time and insisted she take a trifold brochure featuring a sunrise. She told them "No," but they didn't want to hear it. There was something about a woman saying no that struck many as offensive or unconvincing.

That was certainly the case with the meatman, her fourth visitor. He was balding, but what hair he had was the color of corn silk. He had a sharp, elfin face that made it hard to tell whether he was twenty-five or forty. "I hope you haven't been waiting long," she said, not trying to hide the sarcasm in her voice, for he had rung the bell for five minutes and then peered in a window, spotting her in the kitchen.

"You were worth waiting for," he said. He was grossly thin. He wore khakis that were too big for him but cinched to fit his waist by a braided belt.

"Whatever you're selling, I don't want it," she said, but he made no move to leave. His company-issued shirt read Pete's Meats across the breast in red lettering. A black truck in the driveway carried the same logo. "Are you Pete?" she said, and he said, "Sorry?"

"Pete's Meats," she said.

He had a high, shivery voice. "Oh, no. No, no, no. I'm Ron." His forehead wrinkled in amusement. "Tell you the truth, I'm not sure there even is a Pete."

"But you're here to sell meat?"

"Yes!" His eyes were such a pale blue they appeared scrubbed of color. He didn't blink but stared with an intensity that made her keep her hand on the doorknob. "I drive around until I empty the truck and then restock in Kansas City. This is my second day. No luck yet. But maybe my luck will change with you?" His voice rose desperately at the end of every sentence.

She said, "That's sort of a curious thing. To sell meat door to door."

"It is," he said, "strange." He used his teeth to peel the dry skin from his lower lip. And then his tone shifted as he remembered himself and launched into his commercial, touting the quality of his product. "USDA approved! One hundred percent grass fed, organic, delicious." He shared a catalog with her—one that advertised their chops, steaks, tenderloins with photos and their accompanying prices. "We also have a steak-of-the-month club, if you're interested."

She pushed away the catalog and said she would buy a pork chop. One. That's it. That would get rid of him, and besides, there was nothing else in the fridge but condiments. She could use some protein. She told him—Ron, or was it Rob?—she'd be right back with the money. She did not invite him inside, yet that's where she found him when she returned. He had collected the shrink-wrapped chop from the truck. The warmth of the house made it steam in his hand.

"Did I say you could come in? I didn't," she said in a voice that made him widen his eyes, and he said, "It was cold out."

"You should go."

He seemed not to hear this. "It's a big, old, wonderful house. Isn't it?"

They both looked around—at the high timbered ceiling, the shale floor, the darkly lacquered wainscoting—and she said, "Yes. It is." The space was cavernous and yet somehow felt too full with him here.

A DVD player, a tablet, a laptop, a desktop computer, a printer, a Bose stereo, and maybe fifty CDs were stacked on the couch in a nest of cables. He pointed to them, a question forming on his lips, and she handed over the cash and motioned to the door and said, "Go. Please."

He looked back at the pile of electronics and then at her. "But what are you doing all the way out here in the middle of nowhere?"

"I like to be left alone," she said, and started for the door as if she would leave if he didn't.

He started forward and, with one foot inside the house and one foot out, said, "Is it just you here?"

"Of course not."

"Then where's everybody else?"

"They're here."

"But where?"

She pushed him with the door, forcing him onto the porch, and he lingered there and stared at her through the window and in the silence between them a train whistle sounded its banshee cry.

..

10:30 a.m.—November 20—New Auburn, Wisconsin

In any small town, the funeral director is often the coroner, and the funeral parlor is often the nicest home. This was no exception. Mildred had inherited the business—Clary Memorial Services—from her father. Three stories with a mansard roof and a wrap-around porch and ivy threading the brick walls. She lived alone. She had wanted to marry, and came close several times, but the men inevitably complained about the bodies in the basement, the smell of death on her fingers. Undertaking was an odd thing for a woman to do—they said; wouldn't she consider something else?

She wouldn't. If they didn't like it, to hell with them. She committed herself to her job alone, speaking in a hushed voice, smiling kindly, a tissue never far from the hand as she spoke about grave sites and cremation receptacles and what hymns might be appropriate for the service. She always wore an ankle-length dress—black or gray or dark blue—no matter if she visited the supermarket or a Rotary fund-raiser. She was tall with a long face and kept her silvering hair tied always in a tight braid.

She had seen the insides of too many people. The biological failures of the body and the inelegant finality of death had made her long ago give up on God. But she still went to church. It was expected of a woman in her position. And the rituals gave her some calming pleasure. This Sunday—as the organ wheezed and she took the wafer on her tongue and returned to her pew—she noted, not for the first time, the emptiness of the sanctuary.

The few in attendance were gray haired, like herself. Supported by canes and walkers. Their skin spotted and their knuckles squared with arthritis. The church was dying. The town was dying. And she was helping it along its way. No car exited the freeway except to get gas, and no train stopped except to collect grain. Sometimes at night, from the window of the funeral home, she looked out on the town and imagined the homes as moonlit tombs.

When the service ended, she found the sheriff waiting for her in the parking lot. He had a round belly and a thick mustache and leaned against his Bronco with his thumbs hooked into his belt. "Got a stiffie for you, Mildred," he said. "Don't go misconstruing that as sexual harassment."

"Who is it?"

"We're not sure," he said. "Not sure where it came from either. Pulled off the top of a railcar. Could be it crossed state lines, and if so, might have to get the feds involved. Already got the damned railroad police on the phone."

"I didn't know there was such a thing," she said, "as railroad police."

She was taller than him, and whenever they were close, he stiffened his posture to compensate. He swung open the rear door so that they could see in the back, a black-bagged body like a pupa. "Yeah, well. They're on their way. Probably in an Amtrak with rack lights and a siren."

"Maybe we shouldn't do this here," Mildred said and looked around, but the rest of the congregation remained inside the church, nibbling on cookies and sipping decaf.

The sheriff yanked the zipper and peeled open the bag and said, "I won't keep you from your dungeon. Just take a look at this, though, would you?"

At first Mildred thought it was a boy, but it was a man. Blond and balding. Maybe thirty-five. She could always tell someone's age from their neck. The wrinkles and elasticity of the skin. His was going green and purple, the way the sky did after sunset. "Twelve hours, I'd guess," she said.

Mildred always kept a jar of Vicks in her purse and she smeared some beneath her nose before leaning in, masking the smell. "I can't say for sure, not until I open him up, but I'm guessing this is what killed him." She traced a sunken section of skull, a bit of brain poking through the seams. "Blunt force. Brick, baseball bat, rifle butt. Somebody came up behind him and let him have it."

His mouth appeared sunken. Mildred hooked a finger inside it. "The teeth have been removed, but the lips are relatively intact, so I'd guess pliers. Not a lot of blood staining the face, so he was already dead during the extraction."

The sheriff opened the bag farther to reveal arms that ended at the wrists. "Give me a hand, would you?" His teeth showed in a smile beneath his mustache. "Get it?"

"Cleanly cut. Also bloodless." Mildred pulled away from the shadowed hold and stepped into the sun. The bells began clanging in the church tower to mark the noon hour, and the sound chased some pigeons away.

"Why the hell would somebody do something like that?" the sheriff said. "Just a sicko, I guess."

"No," Mildred said. She did not see the body as sacred but as a mere envelope sacking its many parts together. Two things had been taken from it and with a clear purpose. "They wanted to buy themselves time to get away."

··

4:16 p.m.—November 24—Steele County, Minnesota

The Templetons couldn't believe it. After more than twenty-four hours of travel—Brussels to London to New York to Minneapolis to Sioux Falls—they wanted nothing more than to throw down their bags and collapse into bed. But the house was not as they had left it.

Susan was the first to notice. The pan on the stove, a bit of char and grease still clinging to it, along with the dirtied plate and silverware in the sink. She hated coming home to a dirty house. She had polished the kitchen to a glow before they set off on their vacation two weeks ago. That's when she said, "Hal?"

He was pouring himself a short glass of whiskey. His hair mussed. His eyes swollen with fatigue. He didn't bother saying, What? He was beyond language. He just looked at her, waiting.

"I think someone's been in our house."

The emergency dispatcher told them to leave, just to be safe, so they waited for the police at the end of their gravel driveway, among the bare apple trees, skeletal with the onset of winter. Ten minutes later a tan cruiser pulled up with two deputies in it. They walked the property, toured the house, poking under beds and in closets, before waving the Templetons inside.

There were no open drawers or broken lamps or overturned bureaus. The house was as they had left it, except missing all of its art and jewelry and electronics. Hal's rifle cabinet was empty. So was the drawer in the night table where he kept his 9mm and wristwatches. From the dining room the thief had even taken the Tiffany chandelier, a few wires spidering from the empty fixture.

There were small variations between the deputies—one an inch taller, the other with thicker eyebrows—but otherwise they appeared to be the same white, twentysomething, close-shaven, broadshouldered man. One of them showed the Templetons the rear sliding door, its broken lock. "So this appears to be where he entered," and hardly a breath passed before the other said, "But the curious thing is, an upstairs window also appears to have been jimmied."

Most robberies, they explained, were crimes of opportunity. A cell phone glowing on a restaurant table. A purse dangling loosely from a shoulder. An open window. An unlocked car. These are the grab and gos. They're sloppy, dumb, mean. "But this?" one of the deputies said. "This was a professional."

The professionals plan. They cover their tracks. They often begin with the phone book, making note of all the doctors, dentists, lawyers, accountants, veterinarians in an area. Even if their home address isn't listed in the white pages, the deep Web has crawlers that can help. From there they study social media accounts. Usually someone was on vacation, posting photos of a pig roast on a beach in Hawaii or a white-humped mogul field in Colorado.

Hal heaved a sigh, and Susan rubbed his shoulders and said, "At least no one was hurt. Thank God for that at least."

That was when the deputies looked at each other. "Did you have a dog, Mrs. Templeton?" one of them said. "Or perhaps a cat?"

"Cats," the other said. "It would have to be cats—plural—to account for that much blood."

"I'm sorry, what?" Susan said, looking back and forth between them. "What are you talking about?"

"Do you have any pets?" the deputies said.

"No. Hal's allergic to dander. What's this about blood?"

The deputies led them to the furnace room and paused at the door. One of them said, "The good news is, there's no body," and the other one said, "And the bad news is, there's a shitload of blood."

..

2:00 a.m.—November 20—Saint Paul, Minnesota

There is a pawnshop below every pawnshop. All you have to do is ask for the secret drawer. Most of the sales go online—on the dark Web, with Bitcoins, through anonymous Tor servers—where you sell and buy an Omega wristwatch that smells like somebody else's cologne, a smartphone with its SIM card plucked, a Beretta with the microstamping filed from the breech face and firing pin.

Jimmy worked the register—dealing with the deadbeats trying to pawn their neighbor's lawnmower, their grandpa's box TV—but made most of his money online. The shop was a cinder-block bunker with barred windows that sat behind a vacant strip club called the Double Deuce. He wore a different tracksuit every day of the week and shaved his whole body every morning. He liked the way it made him feel clean.

The query came to him through a wiki he'd set up. Suspect Zero, that was the name on the Hushmail account. After some back-and-forth—digital photos, some gentle bartering—they arranged a date and time. After hours, he waited at the door for the knock. Three times fast, one slow. He unlocked everything but the chain and blinked his surprise. A woman stood on the other side of the crack. "You're my contact?" he said. "Suspect Zero?"

She wore a motorcycle jacket with a belt around the middle, a blond wig, and big black sunglasses like some movie star you see in the tabloids. "That's me."

"What's your name?"

"Maybe it's Laura. Maybe it's Linda. Or maybe it's mind your fucking business."

"Fine, fine." He held up his Ruger, not as a threat, just to show, then tucked it in his jeans and loosed the chain and stepped outside into the chill November air. "Let's see what you brought me."

The truck read Pete's Meats across its boxy refrigerated compartment. She opened the rear doors to show off a neatly arranged space crammed not with sirloin but DVD players, laptops, flatscreens, tablets, smartphones. The spoils of how many houses? Maybe five, maybe twenty—he wasn't asking questions. A lot of work and risk went into something like this if she was operating alone. Casing an address, timing the break-in, dealing with dogs and security and neighbors, maybe even the owners themselves. It takes time to clean out a house properly, and you've got to be willing to hurt anybody who gets in your way.

He let out a long, low whistle and examined an espresso machine. To it she had adhered a sticky note carrying the agreed-upon price. "You're a professional," he said, and she said, "Let's get this done with." He took a quick inventory, and she closed the door and locked it and held out the key. "Yours, once you transfer the Bitcoins to my account." A train cried somewhere in the night, and she tipped her head to listen to it.

They went inside, and he split open his laptop for her to view. Jimmy logged on through Tor and readied a transfer. Just as he was about to strike the enter key, he raised his eyebrows, the only hair he kept on his body. "I could make it more, you know."

"Could you?"

"Pete's Meats," he said with a smile curling his mouth. "You want to sell me some hams? Some thighs? Some breasts? You know what I'm saying?"

"No."

"No? You sure?" He traced his lower lip with his thumb. "Another thou? You look worth it."

She hadn't removed her sunglasses, though the lights were low. Her face was as expressionless as a mask. She reached out a hand for his and gripped it firmly. "Yeah?" he said. "You know what I'm saying?" She guided his hand toward the keyboard and his finger depressed the enter key, completing the transfer.

Then she leaned in, so that his reflection warped in her sunglasses, and said, "No."

He didn't like the way she said the word—like she was spitting it, like he gave her mouth a bad taste—so he said, "Maybe I'm not asking." He wasn't sure if he meant it or not, but he wanted to take back control. This was his shop, for fuck's sake. "Where are your manners? You can't even kiss the guy who bought you dinner?"

Her hand was already in his, and he twisted it one way, then the other, trying to shake some emotion out of that dead face of hers, but nothing. She was giving him nothing.

She looked up—he guessed at the security camera—and then back at him. "What?" Jimmy said. "You worried about who's watching? I'm watching. Who are you, anyway? With your stupid costume. Giving me shit in my store."

Her other hand had remained in her pocket all this time. Now it emerged in a flash, and he realized too late she was gripping a knife. Its point bit through his wrist and jammed through the other side, lodging into the counter. He screamed and reached for his gun, but she had ripped it from his belt and knocked him across the mouth with its butt. A hot rolling ache overcame his body and made him hers.

Already Jimmy understood—before she demanded the key code, before she emptied the safe, before she destroyed the security feed, before she dulled him with a blow to the temple and left him pinned to the counter and shoved the truck keys in his mouth— that she was in fact the blade and not the meat to be butchered.

The Dummy

She was pretty enough for a man, handsome enough for a woman. That's what people said about her. She cut her hair short and feathered it up with gel. Her jaw was long and bunched with muscles. Her eyes seemed to squint even when there was no sun. She was thin but not slight, tightly roped with muscle, with wide shoulders set in a constant slouch, maybe because she had bad posture or maybe because she was hiding her breasts. For a laugh she sometimes called them her mosquito bites, because she knew making a joke at her own expense took away the power of those who might try to hurt her. She hated that she lived like this, always guarding against an ugly look, a cruel word, or worse. Her parents named her Johnette.

In high school she wrestled. No one encouraged her to do so, least of all her parents, but she liked the purity of it, a true sport, one body against another. Everyone always said the real wrestlers belonged to the lower weight classes. Anybody athletic over 160, 170 ended up poached by football, baseball, basketball. She wrestled at 120 and did all right in her first season, with a 31–15 record, though many of her wins came when an opponent abstained from a match, refusing to wrestle a girl.

She hated that word. *Girl*. Only four letters, but crammed into it was a whole lexicon of curses flavored with lavender, bubble gum, and baby powder. It wasn't her word, but people kept trying to staple it to her. She hated the word *she*, too, but she hated more the annoyance and cross-eyed confusion that came when she test-drove the pronoun *they* for a few weeks. She didn't fit her body, and her body didn't fit language. The world sometimes felt like a clothing store where shirts were called pants and pants were called sweaters and everything was itchy and sized incorrectly and meant to cause discomfort.

The team practiced on dummies named Bill. The school owned five of them. At the beginning of practice the coach would swing open the supply closet and snap on the light and the Bills would be waiting in a shadowy huddle. They could stand upright. They were made of black nylon. They weighed the same as her, 120 pounds. They had squared heads and rounded fists. They looked like scarecrows dressed head to toe in S&M leather.

Strikes, submission, throws, takedowns. Again and again, she would hurl the Bills to the mat. An arm drag. A duck under. Those were her favorite moves, the moves that didn't require as much strength, the moves that played off the balance and weight of the opponent.

Her coach was a short old man with enormous hands and a neck so wide he had to scissor a slit in the collar of the gray sweatshirts he always wore. He said you didn't wrestle for the trophies, you didn't wrestle for the matches—you wrestled for the drills—and if you didn't take pleasure in the pain and drudgery of it all, you should go home. Some did, but not Johnette.

Why call the dummies Bill, she asked him, why not Frank, Steve, Joe? He said back in the day, that's how the dummies came, as legless bodies with "BILL" printed across their chests. She liked the idea of the old Bills better. She imagined them as rice sacks with noodley arms stitched onto them. Something obviously lifeless. Not like these Bills, who stood at odd angles and made moaning, squelching noises against the mats and smelled like the sweat smeared across them daily and seemed sometimes to be gazing at her.

Of course there were those who thought it wrong for her to wrestle, the worst among them a boy named Breck. He wrestled at 190, too slow for football. He drank protein shakes and energy drinks. His breath smelled like the water in a vase full of rotting flowers. Sometimes they sparred together. He liked to bring an elbow to her throat, a knee to her groin and comment on what he didn't find there. He kept his hair shaved down to the consistency of a wire brush he used to scrape her. Every now and then he tried to grow a failure of a mustache. When he was a boy, Breck overturned a fryer full of hot grease that cooked his left arm completely, the fingernails peeling away, the skin sloughing off like a snake's, all the way to his shoulder, replaced by scar tissue the color of an angry sunburn. He claimed the arm could feel no pain and to prove his point would prod at it with the tip of a compass or hold a lit Zippo beneath his elbow until it blackened.

Sometimes she felt the same way about her mind. She was not capable of the same sort of injury as others. As if there was something already dead about her. Killing never bothered her. Maybe it even felt a little good to lash out at a world that seemed so intent on hurting her. She shot crows and robins from branches with a slingshot. She chased down grasshoppers and pinched them between her fingers and stared at the black spit that swelled from their mouths—and then she would toss them into spiderwebs and watch them struggle and tangle and eventually go still when a spider danced down and filled them with poison and stitched them into a white sack. A river ran through town, and she would gather frogs from its banks and hurl them high and watch their legs spread as if they might learn to fly. They never did. The cement smacked the purplish guts from them.

She asked her coach if she might take one of the Bills home—she knew she needed to work harder if she wanted to make it to state— and he said all right, so long as she brought the dummy back in one piece. She arranged the Bill in the passenger seat of the old Ford truck she drove and buckled him in so that he wouldn't lean on the sharp curves. They drove together around town in this way, his black shape beside her like a shadow.

She lived in a neighborhood near the downtown, where bungalows crowded together and oak trees made shady tunnels with their branches and buckled the sidewalks with their old roots. Her house had a two-story detached garage, and from the second story she swept away the dirt and cleared away the old boxes and storm windows and laid down mats and made it into a wrestling room. There were a few dumbbells lying around, a pull-up bar she'd drilled between the exposed rafters. After dinner—after she cleared the dishes from the table and rushed through her homework—she dragged the Bill upstairs and practiced a Granby, a double arm bar, a gut wrench, a cradle. Only after committing these moves hundreds of times, her coach said, would she have the instinct, the muscle memory she needed.

One night, when she had brushed her teeth and pulled on her pajamas and went to drop the shades, she saw she had left the light on in the garage, its second-story window aglow, much of it filled with the black, slumped silhouette of the Bill. She could not help but feel he was watching her. She remembered a show about the occult she had seen on the History Channel. The narrator had said that anything in a human shape took on a human essence. That was the principle behind a golem, a voodoo doll, a wicker man. Johnette did not think much of this then, but wondered now.

When Breck discovered she was taking a Bill home on nights and weekends, he began calling the dummy her boyfriend. She was the only girl on the team—she wished there was another stupid word for her—but she did enjoy having a locker room all to herself. One time, after she padded across the tile and cranked the hot water on the shower and soaped and rinsed her body and wrapped herself in a towel, she saw her Bill propped against the lockers. He was dressed up in a smiley-face tie. A plastic flower was duct-taped to one hand. A purple dildo to the other.

She dressed, and with her hair still wet, marched from the locker room and found Breck and a few other boys sniggering in the parking lot. Without saying a word she shoved him, and he fell back onto the hood of his Camaro with the plastic testicles hanging from the rearview mirror. She said, "You come in that locker room again, I'll make sure you're expelled," and he said, "What? You scared I saw your dick?" and she said, "Try sucking it ten minutes, maybe you could grow a proper mustache."

The other boys laughed at this, but Breck did not.

The problem with Breck was the problem with all men, she decided. The way she looked *confused* them. She did not grow out her hair. She did not wear lipstick or perfume or earrings. Her skin did not look like strawberry ice cream, nor her eyes like hard candy. Most days she wore a too-large T-shirt, but sometimes a collared shirt with a skinny tie. When people asked her why she dressed like that, she said, "Why does there have to be a reason besides *I like it*?" She hated how everyone wanted an explanation for why she was the way she was. Boys studied her uncertainly, as if peeping in a window only to find their reflection in it. They were goofy and bossy when they first met her—then cruel and aloof when they realized she would not fuck them. More than once she had been called a dyke, and maybe she wouldn't mind kissing Samantha Dexter, who sat behind her in Spanish 4, but the word itself felt like some cousin to *girl*: a label meant to deride or pigeonhole her. She didn't know what she was—and she didn't know who she wanted—and she wished people weren't so fixated on figuring her out.

The next day, when she was raking last year's leaves from the yard, a chipmunk scurried from the woodpile. She remained perfectly still until it came near enough to bring the rake down on. It squeaked and struggled and eventually went still. She knew then the same poisoned pleasure Breck must feel when hurting her.

She looked around to see if anyone had seen her. The Bill sat in the passenger side of her truck, like a patch of midnight the sun hadn't swept away. She swung the rake toward him, held out the chipmunk, punctured on a tine, like an offering.

She knew her business with Breck was not over—she knew he would want to punish her further—but she never expected him to come for her at home. Late one night, in the second story of her garage, she accidentally lost her grip on the Bill and gashed him against an exposed nail. She tracked down a roll of duct tape and whispered sorry when she lovingly applied it to the wound at his forehead.

A shoe scuffed the floor behind her.

She spun around, too late, his arm already around her neck, his weight dragging her down. She tore at him, the dead arm that stole her breath, though she knew it would do no good. She wondered if he could not distinguish pain because his skin felt always aflame. She wondered if that matched the feeling inside him now. His arm—when he flipped her over, her back to the mat—made a creaking, rubbery sound that reminded her of the wrestling dummies, the Bills, when she mangled them into submission.

She called out to her Bill then—called out to him as if he could hear her—but the Bill did not answer.

There was only Breck with his dead arm, hovering and gasping over her, and with the light behind him, he had taken on a dark, silhouetted appearance, so that he did not look like himself, but any boy, every boy. He groped at her body, pulled at her clothes. He wanted her to know she belonged to him.

She went silent, lest he mistake her cries for encouragement. She was never as strong as the boys she wrestled, but she could often outmaneuver them and only twice had she been pinned. She had a strong neck and would arc it back to keep her shoulders from lying flat. She did the same now, as if this were just another match, but then he pressed a forearm into her throat and she lay flat. He panted into her face. She could see his tongue. It was yellow, almost colorless.

When she was young, four or five or six, she had liked to linger in the bath until her fingers pruned. To hurry her, her mother would yank the plug and say that Johnette would swirl away with the rest of the water if she didn't scramble out of the tub and into a towel and then bed, where she would dream of whirling downward, into darkness, which is a little what she felt like now.

She was swirling away, almost gone. Blackness pooled at the edges of her eyes, like a tide of unconsciousness about to overtake her, and then it solidified into the shape of a man. He stood over them, watching.

One moment Breck was biting her ear and the next moment he was not. One moment her throat felt crushed by a dull guillotine and the next moment she could breathe. She coughed and gulped for air, her lungs hitching, her body shuddering. Then she cleaned the tears from her eyes and wobbled to her feet. It took her a long minute to make sense of what she saw.

She did not recognize Breck at first. His back was bent in half the wrong way. His mouth was still moving but no sound came out. She guessed he would live, but she wasn't in a hurry to find out. The sight of him did not scare but relieved her. He was like a robin pegged by a slingshot or a chipmunk pronged by a rake. He had lost. Maybe there would be repercussions, but right now the world outside of this room didn't seem to exist.

Against the wall slumped her Bill. His color matched the feeling inside her. Bruise-black. Black as the deepest hole. The duct tape had peeled away to reveal the gash on his forehead. She used her thumb to seal it in place. Then she took the dummy in her arms and rocked him and whispered thank you and kissed the place where a mouth might have been.

Heart of a Bear

The bear did not know he was capable of love. This would come later. Now he knew only hunger from the bait oozing on his chops—and fear from his trap-ruined paw and the sound of dogs baying behind him in close pursuit.

Earlier, a five-gallon bucket of lard-and-honey mash had led him to a clearing. He had knocked it over and lapped at the thick discharge of it until a steel-fanged trap arced out of the grass to swallow his front left paw.

For an hour he yanked at the trap and chewed at the chain that bolted it to the ground. Whimpering, bleeding, he circled the trap's anchor, trying to find some way out of its orbit, but of course there wasn't one.

Then he heard the dogs.

Night was falling. The sky was gray-ceilinged with clouds. The bear could smell snow and the dogs could smell him and their hungry yowling carried through the woods and compelled the bear to lurch back against the chain. With all his strength he ripped and jerked and finally pulled free his paw but not without great injury, his fur and pads and muscles unpeeling like a glove to reveal something thin-fingered and glisteningly red, what could have been mistaken for a hand.

And now he was lumbering through the trees, knocking against them, unbalanced and half-mad with pain. The dogs were nearly upon him when he turned to face them. A swipe of his paw sent a hound spiraling into a tree, where it hit with an unholy yelp. Another he pulled into an embrace and crushed until it dropped limply between his bowed and shaggy legs. Another still he caught in his jaws and gnashed. And then he snarled and lumbered in a circle and raked his claws across the frozen ground once, as if to strike a flame, before discovering he was alone.

He huffed; a cloud of steam rose from his snout.

Snow—the flakes as large as moths—began to fall. It muffled the men's voices, but the bear could still hear them shouting excitedly, moving toward him. He licked his injured paw and gave a low-throated moan, wanting nothing more than to collapse on a bed of pine needles, to rest deeply, but the men were coming and he had no choice but to once again hobble forward. The sun sank behind the mountains, and the clouds appeared as dark and ridged as the walls of a cave. The snow thickened and caused his vision, already bad, to worsen. He did not know where to go, and no matter which way he chose, he would not be able to last much longer.

The wind rose then. Skeins of snow twisted and swirled and made him feel dizzy, adrift. A great horned owl floated silently through the woods, and the bear followed its vanishing shape. Flakes clung to his fur and to the branches of the pine trees he shambled past. When a window—an ice-glittered rectangle of light—burned out of the storm he saw it almost as a doorway lit by the sun, the entrance to a better world.

The house was a one-story ranch and beneath its porch one of the latticed sections had fallen over and was tangled with browned weeds and frosted with snow. The bear spotted the opening and dragged his body through it and found there a burrow among the rotting mulch and mouse pellets and the bones and moldering feathers of cat-killed birds.

Through the night the snow continued to fall, covering his tracks, and the wind continued to blow, carrying away his scent, and the bear chose this place then to convalesce.

Weeks later he woke to light streaming through a recessed window. He was still confused by sleep and felt as though he was deep in a lake and approaching the surface. He blinked several times, yawned widely, clacked his teeth, and licked his chops. He felt an ache in his paw and held it out before him. It was gummed up with scabs that were melting into scar tissue. His mind took some time to process what had happened and where he was, just as his eyes took some time to focus on what lay beyond the frosted glass.

When he saw the people moving inside the house—carrying loads of laundry, exercising with dumbbells—he felt at first nothing but fear. Humans, after all, carried rifles and chainsaws; they owned trucks and dogs that growled. When they came to the forest they left behind fires and candy wrappers and knife-scratched bones. But beneath the porch, surrounded by snowdrifts, the bear felt safe and exhausted and unhurried as he floated in and out of the slow time of hibernation and observed them.

The man was built like an immense slab of stone—with no neck to speak of, his broad shoulders rounding out of his ears and his shovel of a jaw resting directly on his collar. The woman had a willowy build, and her feathery hair fluttered and seemed ready to take wing whenever she moved. They looked wrong together, even to the bear, like a flower caught in the roots of a gnarled tree. Despite this, they somehow seemed to nourish each other, laughing often, hugging and even chasing each other, tangling together on the floor. They had a baby, a girl. She had a round face and a black thatch of hair. Her milk-white skin along her arms and legs creased over with fat. When she wasn't eating or napping she was crawling about the house and shoving things into her mouth.

Over the next few months, the bear felt something magical take hold of him as he watched them, first in the basement, later through their living room and bedroom and bathroom windows. They never closed the blinds—woods surrounded the house, and they thought themselves unobserved. He watched them when they cooked dinner and exercised and made love and sat before the television. And as he watched, the bear could feel something inside him changing. For the first time, he was aware of more than simple, blind urges—hunger, shelter, sex—and began to turn inward. He really had no idea who he was, not yet, but hidden beneath the layers of fur and fat and muscle there was *someone*, all right. A self. A light flared in the darkness inside him; he was like a cave that had not yet been explored.

At night he would crawl from under the porch and practice walking upright. At first he wobbled and stumbled, but then he began to find his balance, a regular, plodding gait he thought respectable. He also tried to speak—with a guttural clumsiness—flopping his tongue, pinching his lips, trying to discover the noises he overheard them making. His heart always hurt when at the end of the night they shut off the lights and in the dark windows he saw nothing but his own reflection.

The husband worked as a handyman. He wore flannel shirts and blue jeans and canvas jackets. He drove a red pickup with toolboxes in its bed. He smelled like oil and lumber. He often came home with sawdust in his hair and grime beneath his fingernails. To his daughter he made silly faces and spoke in a high, singsongy voice that did not suit his size.

Sometimes he would come home from work and go to the living room and pull the coffee table off the rug before rolling it halfway over to reveal a certain off-color floorboard that he would pry up with a knife. Beneath, he kept a pistol and a shoebox full of money. He would add a few bills to it now and then. He called this their Hawaii trust. Hawaii, the bear came to understand, was a kind of dream that was a long way off.

And at the end of every day—when the man walked through the house and shut off all the lights, when the rooms collapsed into darkness and for several minutes the bear could still see a ghostly glimmering in his eyes and then that, too, was gone, when there was only the black jawline of the forest and above that the night sky spattered with stars whose meager light lit his way when he crawled to his burrow beneath the porch—he understood that their lives had become a kind of Hawaii to him.

One day, after the winter's worth of snow had melted, after the sun had burned through the clouds and dried out the mud-slime that coated the earth, the bear decided he would introduce himself to the woman. He had had a dream about her the night before. In it, she ran her hands through his fur and rubbed his belly and stared into his eyes.

He waited for the man to climb into his pickup and rumble off to work, and then the bear crawled out from under the porch and punched the doorbell and heard its chime echo through the house, heard her footsteps thudding toward him, and then the door opened and she was standing there in a T-shirt and pajama pants, a glass of milk in her hand.

He had watched her so long that on some level, he felt she should already know him. He was about to tell her hello when she dropped the milk. It shattered on the tiles, a white starburst. A stream of it ran along the grouting—toward the door, the bear—and for a moment the woman stared down at it before she screamed and ran into the kitchen and yanked a cleaver from the butcher block. Her hair was pulled back in a ponytail that seemed to pull back her face with it, her eyes wide and teeth bared.

He was close behind her, trying to calm her, telling her, "No, no, no" in his gruff, barking way. But she could not understand him, could not understand that he meant her no harm, and she slashed at him with the cleaver and opened up a gash on his outstretched arm.

His anger took over then. That old rage that guided him in the woods. For a moment the pattering of blood was the only sound. Then he took in a big gulp of air and released a roar that knocked her back a step and filled her face with terror and thundered through the house and shook the pictures on the walls, the glasses in the cabinets. And then he ate her.

He pleasured in the taste, as she had betrayed and insulted him. He had come to believe he was like her, and her rejection had spoiled that belief. A lunch pail sat forgotten on the counter. The bear noticed this when he rose from the floor and wiped his dripping maw with a dishcloth. He heard, then, the engine puttering up the driveway. Tires chewed over gravel. Boots clomped up the porch.

When the man pushed through the half-open door and complained good-naturedly about his wife letting the flies in, the bear surprised him with a swing of the paw that broke his neck before he could even register the blood and viscera glopping the kitchen linoleum.

The baby woke from her nap and began to wail. For a long time the bear listened to the rise and fall of her crying. As if in response, a breeze came rushing from the woods and pushed the door open farther, causing its hinges to creak and permitting sunlight to stretch across the floor and touch the cheek of the dead man. A fly landed on his eye and buzzed its wings. The bear took a step toward the door, and then slowly toward the hallway. The baby continued to cry—blubbering now, big, wet whimpers. He felt his temper softening.

He had not meant for any of this to happen, and in his fury he had forgotten about the baby. Hearing her now brought a sore feeling to his chest, a heaviness to his eyes. Her crying became the only thing, a presence that threw its arms around him and dragged him down the hall to the bedroom with the pink walls and the white wooden crib in which stood, shaking the bars, howling, the baby.

The bear filled up the doorway. He had to duck his head to step through it. His paw prints carried blood in them, and the floorboards creaked beneath his weight. When the baby spotted him, she immediately stopped crying. She rubbed one eye. Snot hung off the end of her nose. Her chin quivered. The bear was close to her now. He could reach out and snatch her with his paw if he wanted.

He wondered if she would begin crying again and what that would mean, what he would have to do.

Instead her cheeks bunched up in a smile, and she said, "Da da da da."

His paw, without its pads and fur, had healed into something quite flexible. He could pick up stones and toss them. He could turn a doorknob. He could pull open a bathroom cabinet and remove from it a razor and shaving cream. He could knob on the hot water. And he could, with care, shave the fur from his muzzle.

He patted his face dry and studied his reflection in the mirror. This was the first time he had ever seen himself outside of a shadow darkening their windows or a tremulous image reproduced in pond-water. He tried twisting his face into different expressions. When he smiled, revealing a mouth full of sharp teeth and black gums, he realized how monstrous he must appear to humans. He compressed his lips and narrowed his eyes and puffed out his cheeks and thought he now looked at least a little presentable.

The bear remembered the way the mother made the bottle—dumping in several spoonfuls of powder, shaking it up with water—and he did the same now to feed the baby whenever she bawled. For his own hunger he pulled food from the fridge and snacked on the body he had heaved into the basement.

He set the baby in front of the television to keep her occupied, and she burbled and cooed at the images that played across the screen. He felt equally mesmerized. This was their routine over the next few days. He did not bother with diapers and clothes and the floor grew slick with her waste, but neither of them minded. At night he would stand over the baby while she slept, her round head cratering the pillow, her closed eyes trembling with dreams. Her chest would rise and fall with each breath, and to him it sounded like a breeze sighing through cottonwoods, the very essence of peacefulness, as if she didn't have a care in the world.

He wasn't sure but he thought he might miss that feeling, a very animal feeling, lost to him now.

Then they ran out of baby food. The bear gave her everything he could find—cans of soda, a moldering orange, a stale bag of potato chips, the rind at the bottom of a bag of bread. She pushed them all away. He tried water from the tap but this did not seem to satisfy the baby, and her skin began to yellow and the fat melted off her arms and legs. When she sobbed, her face went red and tears raced down her cheeks and her chest hitched—and the bear paced back and forth in a panic.

Finally, after many fitful days, he went to the master bedroom—his bedroom now—and nudged open the closet. A pair of overalls barely fit around him. Over them he pulled a canvas jacket, and though it would not zip, it fit snugly, ripping only a little at the seams. From a hook he removed a hat and yanked it down over his ears.

Then he went to the living room and rolled back the rug and found the place where the floorboards tipped and removed from it the shoebox stuffed with money. The gun he tossed aside.

The bear tried to remember what he had learned from the television. He turned the key and pulled the gearshift and stomped alternately on the brake and the accelerator before figuring out how to trundle down the driveway and onto the highway. He huffed with excitement. His hand—not a paw, not anymore—gripped the steering wheel tightly. Traffic rumbled around him. Pale faces stared at him from behind car windows. Semis downshifted, sounding like big animals out of breath.

He recognized the Albertsons from the commercial that cycled constantly during daytime soaps. The parking lot was too hot and the grocery store was too cold and he rattled his cart up and down the narrow aisles feeling claustrophobic, disoriented by the competing smells, the abundance of food stacked everywhere, the fluorescent lights glaring from above and reflecting off the white tile below. He began to grab everything he saw, dragging his paw along the shelves and filling the cart to capacity. Then he realized he had forgotten what he had come for and bombed up and down the aisles, the labels streaking by, until at last he found the containers of formula with the blond teddy bear on them. He balanced several of them on top of the pile of groceries already collected.

At the register stood a thin-necked man with a spider tattoo on his forearm. He was staring at the bear. All around him, people were staring. Everyone in the store, he suddenly realized, was motionless, their eyes fixed on him. No one said a thing. Muzak played from the sound system. In a panic the bear shoved the shoebox full of money at the man and raced his cart out the door, leaving a litter of potatoes and hamburger and canned corn behind.

He had passed a park on his way in and out of town, and a few days later he took the baby there because that was what the fathers did on television. A few parents gossiped and played with their children, but when they saw the bear they quietly gathered up their strollers and diaper bags and departed. He did not think they recognized him for what he was—not with his clothes and his upright posture, they couldn't, could they?—but they knew him to be somehow abnormal. He was not one of them—and their recognition of this only made him hate and envy them all the more.

The baby crawled through the grass and the sandbox and the bark dust and stopped occasionally to suck on a dandelion or throw a fistful of dirt. The bear watched the baby—watched her slobbering and babbling and eating everything within her reach, naked and sitting happily in a pool of her own excrement—and the sight reminded him of his time in the forest, when things were simpler, mindlessly pleasurable, his tongue and his nose telling him where to go, what to do.

He felt an ache inside him and wanted very badly to get down on all fours alongside the baby and paw at the dirt and lick up the uncovered worms or tear at a tree and breathe deeply of its resin.

But then a woman on a bicycle went rolling by and he nodded to her and straightened his posture and said, "Good day," in a voice louder than he intended.

At home the bear and the baby would sit on the couch and the light of the television would play over their bodies. They would watch game shows, talk shows, soap operas, police dramas, basketball games, the news. The bear would study people the size of long-legged insects walking back and forth across the screen and he would learn from them patterns of language and behavior.

He wished he were like them. He wished he had a job and a family and friends that he could have picnics with or ride boats with or play basketball with, somebody. But there was only the baby. He did the best he could with her. Sometimes he would try out a line of dialogue or mimic the hand gesture of an actor, and the baby would laugh and clap her fat little hands.

He found a pack of Marlboros in the woman's purse and tried smoking them. The cigarettes kept his lips compressed, his teeth concealed. And the smoke seeping from his mouth formed a cloud that kept him half-hidden. Just one more bit of camouflage, along with the clothes and hats, to distract people from his hulking size.

He wondered if he should apply for a job. He could imagine himself in an office somewhere, telling people what to do.

One day he watched a show on the Discovery channel about a man who had been raised by wolves. There was a shot of him in a white room with too much light. His hair and his beard were long and knotted with mud and sticks. He was loping about on all fours. The camera zoomed in on his face to show his eyes wild and rolling and his mouth lost behind his beard— then the man opened his mouth and howled a song the bear thought he vaguely recognized.

They ran out of baby food again. The baby could be consoled only by sucking on her thumb, a taste of peace. The bear had no money, but he did have the gun.

He waited for the sun to set before he drove again to the grocery store, because television had taught him that robberies take place at night. He sat in the parking lot until it was nearly empty. Beyond the glass-fronted entrance he could see the thin-necked man standing at a register, staring off into nothing. The pistol rested on the console. His long-fingered paw fit around its grip. It was as heavy as a stone. He shoved it in his coat pocket.

The lamps buzzed above him as he stepped from the truck and shuffled through the parking lot, the sliding doors, and across the glowing expanse of white tile to where the shopping carts were lined up. He yanked one away with a jangle. Before he started down an aisle, he chanced a look over his shoulder. The man at the cash register was watching the bear with his eyes and his mouth wide open.

He knew where to go this time. Off the shelves he swept containers of formula and jars of mashed peas and carrots and sweet potatoes. They crashed into the cart until it was full and dripping with the sticky contents of the containers that had burst open. He hurried toward the register, where the man was waiting for him. The bear imagined taking a bite out of his long throat when the lump in the middle of it went up and down and he asked, "Is that some kind of costume?"

The bear did not say anything but held up the pistol. The man knew what to do. He opened the register and filled a paper sack with money and a stream of piss went dribbling down his leg and the bear felt delight at the smell of it, at his power over the man.

At this moment there seemed to be no moral implications. To snatch money from the register was no different from clawing grubs from a log or honeycomb from a bees' nest. The only law of the forest was hunger and its satisfaction.

In the parking lot, he heaved the cart into the back of the pickup and jumped into the cab and drove away at a reckless speed and lay on the horn for the music it made. Cars swerved off the road to avoid him. He could hear the groceries rattling around in the back.

He was laughing, a fast pant that fogged the windshield so that he
had to stick his head out the window to find his way home.

Nights, sprawled out on the king-size bed, he did not fall asleep
right away but stared at the ceiling. He couldn't stop thinking. There
was too much going through his head. His mind felt like a spring-
time river glutted with silt, half-rotted logs, winter-killed beaver.
He wanted to thrust a paw into his mouth and clean out his skull.

He had always felt that he followed the world, but now he had
the strange and growing sense that the world followed him—as if
he were a kind of axis to which it was bolted, turning around and
around him. Maybe this was what made his mind so exhaustedly
busy: all the possibilities and expectations that came with the desire to control, the hunger for knowledge, the weight of responsibil-
ity, the crush of the human mind.

The bear flipped through books. He dug through drawers and
cupboards and closets. He didn't know what he was looking for, not
exactly. The artifacts of a life. The things humans collect to define
themselves. He was hungry not just for answers but for questions.

One evening, when he was digging through boxes in the basement, sniffing at mildewy clothes and studying faded photo albums, there came from upstairs the sharp report of a pistol. It was
like a tree snapping against a hard wind. The noise hurtled through
the house and bottomed out into a dark echo that filled the bear
with dread. And then nothing, a silence interrupted by the low
muttering of the television.

The bear did not want to go upstairs. He wanted to stay down in
the basement forever. But something—a dreadful curiosity—drew
him up. He climbed the stairs and shambled down the hallway that
felt as long and dark as a stone canyon. In the living room, beyond
the coffee table but before the television, he found waiting for him
the smoking pistol and, next to it, the baby.

Its skin was so white where it wasn't red. Its eyes were open but
unseeing. The bear picked it up—yes, it, sexless now in its death—

and shook it and licked it, tried to revive it, but its body was as limp and mindless as a pillow, and soon he set it aside.

For a long time he stared at the baby. As strong and seemingly unassailable as humans were as a population, they were individually nothing more than puny bodies that could be tossed around like dolls, crushed and torn to pieces, opened up by a prick of metal.

He felt the blood rushing through him, like a river pressed up against an ice dam, then breaking through, a messy, gushing release. He felt his breath come in and out in hoarse gasps. He felt himself, for the first time in a long time, as a body and not a mind. On television a storm ripped apart the Florida coast. A weatherman stood in howling wind and pouring rain and described the devastation. And then the image went dark as the bear lifted the television over his head and hurtled it across the room, and it exploded, a smoldering ruin of glass and wires and plastic.

He upended the coffee table. He tore gouges in the couch from which white foam bulged like striations of fat. He knocked over the fridge with a crash that shook the floor. He bashed the faucet from the sink and water shot to the ceiling and there flattened into a shimmering circle that rained down on him. He ripped pictures off the walls. He brought the pistol to his mouth and gnawed at it until his tooth broke. In this way he went through every room, his throat ragged with screaming, his great shaggy arms slashing this way and that. And then, with nothing left to destroy, he shoved through the door, splintering it from the hinges.

In the yard he swung his arms at nothing. He wanted only to hurl the weight of his anger, to make bloody ribbons of the air. When that exhausted him, he fell to all fours and clawed and chewed at the dirt as if to blame it for being a reminder of what form they would all—whether man or beast, stone or plant—return to eventually. And then he was done, utterly spent and alone. His tongue lolled as he breathed raggedly in the half dark, a muddy line of drool streaming from his mouth.

From the forest came the sound of an owl hooting. Its low-noted voice sounded sad. Or maybe the bear was so sad that everything would seem that way to him, from the reddest sunset to a toad crushed into gravel by a tire.

He looked back at the house. It looked too small to have ever contained him, and it seemed to shrink farther and farther away as he watched it now and understood that he was falling out of one life and into another. He held out his ruined hand toward the house, then let it fall.

He would not resist the pull he felt. He followed his mandate and went crashing and yowling into the dark mouth of the forest to which he belonged.

Dial Tone

A jogger spotted the body hanging from the cell tower. At first he thought it was a mannequin. That's what he told Z-21, the local NBC affiliate. The way the wind blew it, the way it flopped limply, made it appear insubstantial, maybe stuffed with straw. It couldn't be a body, not in a place like Redmond, a nowhere town caught between the Cascade Mountains and the desert flats of eastern Oregon. But it was. The body had a choke chain, the kind you buy at Pet Depot, wrapped around the neck and anchored halfway up the steel ladder that rose twelve hundred feet in the air to the tip of the tower, where a red light blinked. Word spread quickly. And everyone, the whole town, it seemed, crowded around, some of them with binoculars and cameras, to watch three deputies scale the tower and then descend with the body in a sling.

I was there. And from where I stood, the tower looked like a great spear thrust into the hilltop.

Yesterday—or maybe it was the day before—I went to work, like I always go to work, at West TeleServices Corporation, where, as a marketing associate, I go through the same motions every morning. I hit the power button on my computer and listen to it hum and mumble and blip to life. I settle my weight into my ergonomic chair. I fit on my headset and take a deep breath, and, with the pale light of the monitor washing over me, I dial the first number on the screen.

In this low-ceilinged, fluorescent-lit room, there are twenty-four rows of cubicles, each ten deep. I am C5. When I take a break and stand up and peer into the cubicle to my right, C6, I find a Greg or a Josh or a Patti—every day a new name to remember, a new hand to shake, or so it seems, with the turnover rate so high. This is why I call everyone *you*.

"Hey, you," I say. "How's it going?"

A short, toad-like woman in a Looney Tunes sweatshirt massages the bridge of her nose and sighs. "You know how it is."

In response I give her a sympathetic smile before looking away, out over the vast hive of cubicles that surrounds us. The air is filled with so many voices, all of them coming together into one voice that reads the same script, trying to make a sale for AT&T, Visa, Alaska Airlines, or Sandals Resorts, among our many clients.

There are always three supervisors on duty, beefy men with mustaches. Their bulging bellies remind me of feed sacks that might split open with one slit of a knife. They wear polo shirts with "West TeleServices" embroidered on the breast. They drink coffee from stainless steel mugs. They seem never to sit down. Every few minutes I feel a breeze at the back of my neck as they hurry by, usually to heckle some associate who hasn't met the hourly quota.

"Back to work, C5," one of them tells me, and I roll my eyes at C6 and settle into my cubicle, where the noise all around me falls away into a vague murmur, like the distant drone of bees.

I'm having trouble remembering things. Small things, like where I put my keys, for instance. Whether or not I put on deodorant or took my daily vitamin or paid the cable bill. Big things too. Like, getting up at 6:00 a.m. and driving to work on a Saturday, not realizing my mistake until I pull into the empty parking lot.

Sometimes I walk into a room or drive to the store and can't remember why. In this way I am like a phantom: someone who can sink into the floor or float through walls and find myself someplace else in the middle of a sentence or thought and not know what brought me there. The other night I woke up to discover I was standing in the backyard in my pajamas, my bare feet blue in the moonlight. My hands held a shovel.

Today I'm calling on behalf of Capital One, pitching a mileage card. This is what I'm supposed to say: Hello, is this _____? How are you doing today, sir/ma'am? That's wonderful! I'm calling with a fantastic offer from Capital One. Did you know that with our no-annual-fee, no-hassle-miles Visa Signature card, you can earn **25 percent more** than regular mileage cards, with 1.25 miles for every one dollar spent on purchases? On top of that, if you make just three thousand dollars in purchases a year, you'll earn **twenty thousand bonus miles!**

And so on.

The computer tells me what to tell them. The bold sections indicate where I ought to raise my voice for emphasis. If the customer tries to say they aren't interested, I'm supposed to keep talking, to pretend I don't hear. If I stray too far from the script and one of the supervisors is listening in, I will feel a hand on my shoulder and hear a voice whispering, "Stay on target. Don't lose sight of your primary objective."

The lights on the tops of cell towers are meant to warn pilots to stay away. But they have become a kind of beacon. Migratory birds mistake them for the stars they use to navigate, so they circle the towers in a trance, sometimes crashing into a structure, into its steadying guy wires, or even into other birds. And sometimes they keep circling until they fall to the ground, dead from exhaustion. You can find them all around our cell tower: thousands of them, dotting the hilltop, caught in the sagebrush and pine boughs like ghostly ornaments. Their bones are picked clean by ants. Their feathers are dampened by the rain and bleached by the sun and ruffled and loosened and spread like spores by the wind.

In the sky, many more birds circle, screeching their frustration as they try to find their way south. Of course they discovered the body. As it hung there, turning in the wind, they roosted on its shoulders. They pecked away its eyes, and they pecked away its cheeks, so that we could see all of its teeth when the deputies brought it down. The body looked like it was grinning.

At night, from where I lie in bed, I can see the light of the cell tower—through the window, through the branches of a juniper tree, way off in the distance—like a winking red eye that assures me of the confidentiality of some terrible secret.

Midmorning, I pop my neck and crack my knuckles and prepare to make my sixty-seventh call of the day. "Pete Johnston" is the name on the screen. I say it aloud—twice—the second time as a question. I feel as though I have heard the name before, but really, that means nothing when you consider the hundreds of thousands of people I have called in my three years working here. I notice that his number is local. Normally I pay no attention to the address listing unless the voice on the other end has a thick accent I can't quite decipher—New Jersey? Texas? Minnesota?—but in this case I look and see that he lives just outside Redmond, in a new housing development only a few miles away.

"Yeah?" is how he answers the phone.

"Hello. Is this Pete Johnston?"

He clears his throat in a growl. "You a telemarketer?"

"How are you doing today, sir?"

"Bad."

"I'm sorry to hear that, sir. I'm calling on behalf of—"

"Look, cocksucker. How many times I got to tell you? Take me off your list."

"If you'll just hear me out, sir, I want to tell you about a fantastic offer from—"

"You people are so fucking pathetic. You are the worst of the worst."

Now I remember him. He said the same thing before, a week or so ago, when I called him. "If you *ever* call me again, you worthless piece of shit," he said, "I will reach through the phone and rip your throat out. That's a promise."

He goes off on a similar rant now, asking me how can I live with myself, if every time I call someone they answer with hatred?

For a moment I forget about the script and answer him. "I don't know," I say. It's an excellent question, one I struggle with every day.

"What the—?" he says, his voice somewhere between panicked and incensed. "What the hell are you doing in my house? I thought I told you to—"

There is a noise—the noise teeth might make biting hurriedly into melon—punctuated by a series of screams. It makes me want to tear the headset away from my ear.

And then I realize I am not alone. Someone is listening. I don't know how—a certain displacement of sound as the phone rises from the floor to an ear—but I can sense it.

"Hello?" I say.

The line goes dead.

Sometimes, when I go to work for yet another eight-hour shift or when I visit my parents for yet another casserole dinner, I want to be alone more than anything in the world. But once I'm alone, I feel I can't stand another second of it. Everything is mixed-up.

This is why I pick up the phone sometimes and listen. There is something reassuring about a dial tone. That low purr, constant and predictable. More and more people are eliminating their landlines and going wireless, but I will never do that. I need the dial tone. It makes me feel connected, part of a larger stream of sound that tributaries the world. No matter if you are in Istanbul or London or Beijing or Redmond, you can bring your ear to the receiver and hear it.

I listen to the dial tone for the same reason people lift their faces toward the moon when in a strange place. It makes them—it makes me—feel oriented, calmer than I was a moment before. Perhaps this has something to do with why I drive to the top of the hill and park beneath the cell tower and climb onto the hood of my Neon and lean against the windshield with my hands folded behind my head to watch the red light blinking and the black shapes of birds swirling against the backdrop of an even blacker sky.

I am here to listen. The radio signals emanating from the tower sound like a blade hissing through the air or a glob of spit sizzling on a hot stove: something dangerous, about to draw blood or catch fire. It's nice.

I imagine I hear in it the thousands of voices channeling through the tower at any given moment, a digital switchboard, and I wonder what terrible things could be happening to these people that they want to tell the person on the other end of the line but don't.

A conversation overheard: "Do you live here?"

"Yes."

"Are you Pete Johnston?"

"Yes. Who are you? What do you want?"

"To talk to you. Just to talk."

Noon, I take my lunch break. I remove my headset and lurch out of my chair with a groan and bring my fists to my back and push until I feel my vertebrae separate and realign with a juicy series of pops. Then I wander along my row, moving past so many cubicles, each with a person hunched over inside it—and for a moment West TeleServices feels almost like a chapel, with everyone bowing their heads and murmuring together, as if exorcising some private pain.

I sign out with one of the managers and enter the break room, a forty-by-forty-foot room with white walls and a white dropped ceiling and a white linoleum floor. There are two sinks, two microwaves, two fridges, a Coke machine, and a SNAX machine. In front of the SNAX machine stands C6, the woman stationed in the cubicle next to mine. A Looney Tunes theme apparently unifies her wardrobe, since today she wears a sweatshirt with Sylvester on it. Below him, blocky black letters read, WITHCONTHIN. She stares with intense concentration at the candy bars and chips bags and gum packs, as if they hold some secret message she has yet to decode.

I go to the nearby water fountain and take a drink and dry my mouth with my sleeve, all the while watching C6, who seems hardly to breathe. "Hey, you," I say, moving to within a few steps of her. "Doing all right there?"

She looks at me, her face creased with puzzlement. Then she shakes her head, and a fog seems to lift, and for the first time she sees me and says, "Been better."

"I know how you feel."

She looks again to the SNAX machine, where her reflection hovers like a ghost. "Nobody knows how I feel."

"No. You're wrong. I know."

At first C6 seems to get angry, her face cragging up, but then I say, "You feel like someone is holding you down and poking you in the forehead or the chest over and over and over and over. That finger keeps tap-tap-tapping. Dozens of times, hundreds of times, thousands of times. You can feel the pain adding up, and you want to scream because you know that after a while that finger is going to jab through your skin and crack through your bone and finally dig all the way through you." I go to the fridge labeled A–K and remove from it my sack lunch and sit down at a table. "Something like that, anyway."

An awkward silence follows, in which I eat my ham sandwich and C6 studies me closely, no doubt recognizing in me some common damage, some likeness of herself.

Then C6 says, "Can't seem to figure out what I want," nodding at the vending machine. "I've been staring at all these goodies for twenty minutes, and I'll be darned if I know what I want." She forces a laugh and then says with some curiosity in her voice, "Hey, what's with your eye?"

I cup a hand to my ear, like: Say again?

"Your eyeball." She points and then draws her hand back as if she might catch something from me. "It's really red."

"Huh," I say and knuckle the corner of my eye as if to nudge away a loose eyelash. "Maybe I've got pink eye. Must have picked it up off a doorknob."

"It's not pink. It's red. It's really, really red."

The nearest reflective surface is the SNAX machine. And she's right. My eye is red. The dark, luscious red of an apple. I at once want to scream and pluck it out and suck on it.

"I think you should see somebody," C6 says.

"Maybe I should." I comb a hand back through my hair and feel a vaguely pleasant release as several dozen hairs come out by the roots, just like that, with hardly any effort. I hold my hand out before me and study the clump of hairs woven in between the fingers and the fresh scabs jeweling my knuckles and say to no one in particular, "Looks like I'm falling apart."

Have you ever been on the phone, canceling a credit card or talking to your mother, when all of a sudden—with a pop of static—another conversation bleeds into yours? Probably. It happens a lot, with so many radio signals hissing through the air. What you might not know is, what you're hearing might have been said a minute ago or a day ago or a week ago or a month ago. Years ago.

When you speak into the receiver, your words are compressed into an electronic signal that bounces from phone to tower to satellite to phone, traveling thousands of miles, even if you're talking to your next-door neighbor Joe. Which means there's plenty of room for a signal to ricochet or duplicate or get lost. There are so many words—the ghosts of old conversations—floating around us.

Consider this possibility. You pick up your phone and hear a voice—your voice—engaged in some lost conversation, like that time in high school when you asked Natasha Flatt out for coffee and she made an excuse about her cat being sick. It's like a conversation shouted into a canyon, its words bouncing off walls to eventually come fluttering back to you, warped and soft and sounding like somebody else.

Sometimes this is what my memory feels like. An image or a conversation or a place will rise to the surface of my mind, and I'll recognize it vaguely, not knowing if I experienced it or saw it on television or invented it altogether.

Whenever I try to fix my attention on something, a red light goes on in my head, and I'm like a bird circling in confusion.

I find myself on the sidewalk of a new hillside development called Bear Brook. Here all the streets have names like Kodiak and Grizzly. Around me are two-story houses of a similar design, with freshly painted gray siding and stone entryways and cathedral windows rising above their front doors to reveal chandeliers giving off constellations of light. Each home has a sizable lot that runs up against a pine forest. And each costs more than I would make in twenty years at West TeleServices.

A garbage truck rushes past me, raising tiny tornadoes of dust and trash, and I raise my hand to shield my face and notice a number written on the back of it, just below my knuckles—13743— and though I am sure it will occur to me later, for the moment I can't for the life of me remember what it means.

A bird swoops toward a nearby house. Mistaking the window for a piece of sky, it strikes the glass with a thud and falls into the rose garden beneath it, absently fluttering its wings; soon it goes still. I rush across the lawn and into the garden and bend over to get a better look at it. A teardrop of blood runs from its eye. I do not know why, but I reach through the thorns and pick up the bird and stroke its cool, reddish feathers. Its complete lack of weight and its stillness overwhelm me.

When the bird fell, something fell off a shelf inside me—a nice, gold-framed picture of my life, what I dreamed it would be, full of sunshine and ice cream and go-go dancers. It tumbled and shattered, and my smiling face dissolved into the distressed expression reflected in the living room window before me.

I look alarmingly ugly. My eyes are pouched black. My skin is cancer yellow. My upper lip peels back to reveal long, thin teeth. Mine is the sort of face that belongs to someone who bites the heads off chickens in a carnival pit, not the sort that belongs to a man who cradles in his hands a tiny red-winged blackbird. The vision of me, coupled with the vision of what I once dreamed I would be—handsome, wealthy, athletic, envied by men, and cherished by women—assaults me, the ridiculousness of it and also the terror, the realization that I have crept to the edge of a void and am on the verge of falling in, barely balanced.

And then my eyes refocus, concentrating on a farther distance, where through the window I see a man rising from a couch and approaching. He is tall and square shouldered. His hair is the color of dried blood on a bandage. He looks at me with derision.

I drop the bird and raise my hand, not quite waving, the gesture more like holding up something dark to the light. He does not move except to narrow his eyes. There's a stone pagoda at the edge of the garden, and when I take several steps back my heel catches against it. I stumble and then lose my balance entirely, sprawling hard on the lawn. The gray expanse of the sky fills my vision. Moisture from the grass seeps into my jeans and dampens my underwear.

In the window the man continues to watch me. He has a little red mustache, and he fingers it. Then he disappears from sight, moving toward the front door.

As I stagger off the lawn and hurry along the sidewalk, my eyes zero in on the porch, waiting for the man to appear there, and I catch sight of the address: 13743.

And then I am off and running. A siren announces itself nearby. The air seems to vibrate with its noise. It is a police cruiser, I'm certain, though how I can tell the difference between it and an ambulance, I don't know. Either way, someone is in trouble.

The body was blackened by its lengthy exposure to radio frequency fields. Cooked. Like a marshmallow left too long over flame. This is why the deputies shut off the transmitters when they climbed the tower.

Z-21 interviewed Jack Millhouse, a professor of radiation biology at Oregon State. He had a beard, and he stroked it thoughtfully. He said that climbing the tower would expose a person to radio frequencies so powerful they would cook the skin. "I'd ask around at the ER," he said. "See if somebody has come in with radiation burns."

Then they interviewed a woman in a yellow, overlarge T-shirt and purple stretch pants. She lived nearby and had seen the commotion from her kitchen window. She thought a man was preparing to jump, she said. So she came running in the hopes of praying him down. She had a blank, smeary face, like a smashed piece of putty. "It's just awful," she said, her lips disappearing as she tightened her mouth. "It seems like something that should have happened somewhere else, but it's right here."

I know I am not the only one who has been cut off by a swerving car in traffic or yelled at by a teacher in a classroom or laughed at by a woman in a bar. I am not the only one who has wished someone dead and imagined how it might happen, delighting in the goriest details.

Here is how it might happen:

I am in a kitchen with stainless steel appliances and granite counters and a mosaic backsplash that looks like it's made from crushed diamonds. I stand over a man with a Gerber hunting knife in my hand. There is blood dripping off the blade, and there is blood coming out of the man. Gouts of it. It matches the color of his hair. A forked vein rises on his forehead to reveal the panicked beating of his heart. Saliva webs the corner of his mouth. He holds his hands out, waving me away, and I cut through them. He wears a silk shirt. A gold chain flashes at his neck. A watch gleams at his wrist, the same sleek midnight coloring as the Mercedes parked in his garage. He has everything, everything, everything.

A dog barks from the hallway. The man screams in a high, thin, repulsive voice. All of this sounds far away, like a conversation heard through blips of static.

I am aware of my muscles and their purpose as never before, using them to place the knife, aiming it finally at the man's chest, where it will make the most difference.

At first the blade won't budge, caught on a rib, and then it slips past the bone and into the soft red interior, deeper and then deeper still, entering him to the hilt. The response is cathartic: a shriek, a gasp, a stiffening of the limbs followed by a terrible shivering that eventually gives way to a great, calming release.

There is blood everywhere—on the knife, on the floor, gurgling from the newly rendered wound that looks so much like a mouth—and the man's eyes are open and empty, and his sharp pink tongue lolls out the side of his mouth. I am amazed at the thrill I feel.

When I surprised him, only a few minutes ago, he was on the phone. I spot it now, on the shale floor, with a halo of blood around it. I pick it up and bring it to my ear and hope for the familiar, calming murmur of the dial tone.

Instead I hear a voice. "Hello?" it says.

Are you listening? Will you stay on the line just a little longer? Telling the story is complicated. Finding my way to the end and knowing my way back to the beginning without losing my way.

To understand a story like this you would have to know what it's like to speak into a headset all day, reading from a script you don't believe in, conversing with bodiless voices that snarl with hatred, voices that want to claw out your eyes and scissor off your tongue. Do you know what that does to a person? Listening to people scream at me and hang up on me, day after day, with no relief except for the occasional coffee break when I talk with C6 about the television show I watched last night?

I forgot to tell you how Pete Johnston sort of leaned and sort of collapsed against the fridge and a magnet fell to the linoleum with a clack after I slashed the knife in a silvery arc across his face and then his outstretched hand and then into that soft basin behind the collarbone. Something inside me, some internal switch, had been triggered, filling me with an unthinking adrenaline that made me feel capable of kicking a telephone pole to splinters. Again I stabbed the body, in the thigh, the belly, my muscles pulsing with a red electricity.

I am going to offer you a great deal. Low interest rate, no introductory fee. But first you need to know what it felt like to pull the body from the trunk of my car and hoist it to my shoulder. I climbed the tower—one rung, then another—going slowly. From here—thirty, then forty, then fifty feet off the ground—I could see the chains of light on Route 97 and Highway 100, each bright link belonging to a machine that carried inside it a man who could lose control in an instant, distracted by the radio or startled by a deer or overwhelmed by tiredness, careening off the asphalt and into the surrounding woods. It could happen to anyone. It could happen to you.

Imagine for a second that you know what it's like to be me. Your thighs tremble. You are weary, dizzy. Your fillings tingle, and a funny baked taste fills your mouth. The edges of your eyes go white and then crazy with streaks of color. But you continue climbing, with the wind tugging at your body, with the blackness of the night and the black shapes of birds all around you, the birds swirling through the air like ashes thrown from a fire. And let's not forget the sound—the sound of the tower—how it sounds almost like words. The hissing of radio frequencies, the voices of so many others coming together into one voice that courses through you in dark conversation.

Listen.

The Mud Man

Thomas is in his garden when it happens. Weeds choke his daffo-dils, and he hacks at them with his garden claw, breaking up the soil, yanking out clumps to toss in a pail. He isn't concentrating. He is thinking about something else, the problem of a split refund. At this time of year, when everyone crowds his office at once and throws onto his desk rubber-banded 1099s and wrinkly bunches of receipts, he is always thinking about something else—about reduc-tions to the gift tax rate, the new exclusions for estates and trusts, the valuation of qualified real property, and on and on, his mind clogged with numbers and forms, his fingers dirty with ink and crosshatched with paper cuts. "If only I didn't need sleep," he often says to his wife. "If only there were more hours in a day. If only there were two of me."

The garden claw comes down on his hand, two of the tines piercing his glove. It takes Thomas a moment to process the injury. He does not curse—he is not the cursing type—but tears off the glove to account for the damage. The webbing between his thumb and index finger is gashed. And the nail of his middle finger has peeled over, hanging by a red thread. A nub of bone peeks out. The pain arrives a moment later, an electric heat. He can feel his heart beating in his hand. A drop of blood gathers at the tip of his finger, swells fatly, and then falls into the cup of a daffodil.

He likes daffodils more than tulips. You can't count on tulips. You dig so many holes with your spade and arrange the bulbs in a tidy design so that staggered throughout the garden the flowers will appear, blooming in different stages, different colors, Darwin tulips and fringed tulips and parrot tulips and triumph tulips. But things never work out as you expect them to. The squirrels sniff out the bulbs and burrow through the loose soil to chew them like blighted apples. And when spring finally comes, maybe you have a tulip here, a tulip there, scattered survivors soon gnawed down to a serrated edge by a rabbit.

Daffodils are more reliable. Squirrels hate their bulbs, and rabbits their leaves and flowers, for the bitter taste. So daffodils are what he plants, and once their bloom ends, the irises and the daylilies take over, the peonies and columbines and hollyhocks, the hostas, the whole garden color-coordinated, tidily weeded, mapped out perfectly, like the rest of his life.

Next to the toilet sits a magazine rack arranged alphabetically. He folds his socks into neat little balls that run in white, brown, and black stripes through his drawer. Every Saturday he washes his car, a beige Ford Escort, kneeling to pick the bugs from the grille, to scrape any rust specks off the hubcaps. He organizes his grocery list according to aisle. He alternates his mowing patterns—north/south, east/west, diagonal—to ensure the grass doesn't streak with wheel wear.

So the messiness of his hand bothers him more than the pain. He peels off his fingernail and flicks it aside, and it drops into the soil like a seed.

His is a life without music. He finds it distracting, irritating. Even on long car trips he keeps the radio silent, the only noise the hum of the engine, the fizz of the air conditioning. So it is as he drives to the hospital, his hand wrapped in a towel, his mouth tightened into a line as he chews at the insides of his lips and calculates the hours lost to this injury, not just an afternoon in the garden but the weeks ahead in the office, punching numbers, flipping through files.

Later, when he returns home, his hand is gloved in bandages under which his skin is glopped over with Neosporin and stitched up with black string that looks like the coarse sort of hair that might grow on a fly, like the ones that fill the bloody daffodil, buzzing and drinking and making the flower bob and surge with their boiling presence, when once more he stands in his garden, collecting his tools, his gloves, his kneeling cushion.

It is then that he spots, in the very same place he discarded his fingernail, the swollen belly of dirt. Along its edges several flowers lean sideways, displaced. It is cracked along its crown and from the center of it pokes a cluster of green, muddy shoots that look like nothing so much as a handful of fingers, reaching upward. He nudges it with his shoe and mutters, "What the?" but before he can crouch down and observe it more closely, his wife, Rebecca, opens the kitchen window to tell him to please come inside, his Tuesday-night casserole is ready and Owen needs a diaper change and his work phone keeps ringing.

By the next morning, what appears to be a crooked tree, almost an arm—a sinewy tangle of bark and vines and leaves—grows from the garden. Throughout the day it grows larger, and larger still, thickening, branching out, taking on the eventual appearance of a man curled in the fetal position. This is what Thomas observes after work when he rattles the lawn mower out of the garage and into the backyard.

The wind is blowing, and at first Thomas believes it is responsible not only for the trembling of the grass he stands on, but the shivering of the bush. A bush. That is what Thomas—squinting his eyes, cocking his head—processes the hunched shape as, some invasive species of bush. And then he realizes it has its own animation, slowly untangling itself, shuddering to life. In a series of arrested spurts, it straightens from a hunch to the upright position of a man roughly the same height and build as Thomas, round-shouldered, with some thickness about the waist.

He stands in the middle of a shallow crater. His joints issue a series of blistery pops like pitch pockets bursting from a log thrown on a fire. Clods of dirt fall off him and spatter the garden, freckling the daffodils and hostas. He has all the calm of a tree, the breeze rushing around him, bending the loose vines and leaves hanging off him like hair, carrying a smell like worms washed across a sidewalk after a hard rain. The mud man seems to be staring at Thomas, though it is hard to tell, as his eyes are hollows with black scribbles in them, like the insides of a rotten walnut.

When the mud man steps forward, Thomas steps back, so that for a moment they are mirror images of each other. The mud man raises his arm, extending his rooty fingers, and at first Thomas thinks he means to shake hands. But the mud man is instead reaching for the mower. He rips back the cord, and the engine coughs to life. Immediately he sets off across the lawn, making a dark green path all the way to the fence line, where he flips the mower neatly around and continues back toward Thomas, who can only stand there, blinking, scratching vaguely at the itch beneath his bandaging.

His mind is never off the clock, always accounting. He knows how many tiles there are on the floor of his master bath: 15. He keeps a notepad and a pen in his Ford and every time he fills up he calculates his gas mileage: 21, city; 32, highway. He can guess with great accuracy the number of bowel movements he will have in a day based on the dinner he ate the night prior: meat loaf, 1; fish fry, 2; Mexican, 3.5. Before the NCAA tourney, he spends weeks studying stats, injuries, coaching strategies, while composing his bracket. The tidy calculations exhilarate him and inform nearly everything he does, as is the case now, when he glances at his watch and realizes that with the forty minutes saved from mowing the lawn and sweeping its clippings off the sidewalk, he will have time to finish the Anderson Jewelry portfolio before dinner.

The mud man trims the hedges. The mud man lays down fresh mulch. The mud man empties the garbage. At first Thomas tries to keep him out of the house, but the garage needs sweeping and the fireplace is still thick with winter's ashes, so he relents. "I guess it's fine. I could use the help. I'm so busy, I hardly have time to breathe."

The mud man polishes the mildew from the grout in the basement shower stall. The mud man cleans the gutters, pulls out dank fistfuls of leaves, crushes hornets' nests and tosses them aside as if they were balls of dirty paper. The mud man tries to wash the dishes, but gives up after the water darkens and thickens into a kind of gravy.

At first his wife worries. "What will the neighbors think?" she asks. "That I can't take care of our own home? That I'm sitting here all day doing nothing?"

But then, when the mud man brings her a Diet Coke with a slice of lemon, when he picks up Owen's toys, when he irons the wrinkled oxfords that have piled up in the laundry room, when he fixes the satellite so that a jagged line doesn't run down the middle of the television, she begins to grow fond of him, the way he remembers the little things that Thomas doesn't have time for. "I don't know how we got by without you," she says.

Coming home from work and seeing so many tasks completed makes Thomas feel renewed in the world. He smiles and claps the mud man on the shoulder and then goes to the bathroom to scrub the mucky residue off his palm.

Owen is two years old, and Thomas doesn't spend a lot of time with him. Occasionally he tries to play with the boy, piecing together a puzzle or pushing a toy tractor through the sandbox, but they both end up frustrated, because Owen doesn't do things correctly. He fails to put the edges of the puzzle together first. He throws sand into the air and dirties the patio. And Thomas can't help but constantly correct him, saying, "No, no, no," until finally the boy collapses into a red-faced fit.

Thomas knows he should feel guilty about this, but sometimes he forgets Owen even exists. One time he returned home from work and stepped into the kitchen as the garage door rumbled closed and nearly tripped over the boy as he played with his magnets on the refrigerator. "What are you doing here?" he asked, and meant it in more ways than one.

Owen has a large head and short legs. His knuckles are dimpled. His brown eyes match his hair. The boy seems to enjoy the mud man as if he were a pet, something to be chased and pestered. He races between his legs. He plucks leaves off him and tosses them into the air like green confetti. At the end of the day he grabs the mud man by the hand and asks him to help pick out his jammies. The mud man never complains. Thomas even observes him helping the boy up and patting him on the head after a nasty tumble off his tricycle.

This evening, Owen is playing on the living room floor with a plastic dragon the size of a cat. When he pushes a red scale on its back, it stomps forward and opens its jaws and looses a roar. But the batteries are low, so its steps are sluggish and its roar more like the squawk of a strangled bird.

Thomas comes out of his office to get a glass of milk and sees the boy whimpering over the toy. He says, "You wait one minute," and goes to the cupboard where they keep the batteries and a small plastic toolbox and squats down on the carpet next to the boy. "I help," Owen says, and Thomas says, "No. You watch and learn." But his bandaged hand can't grip the dragon properly, and his good hand is cramped from clutching a pen all day and he keeps fumbling the screwdriver, which is too big for the small screw on the dragon's belly, where the batteries are housed. After he bungles the job for the third time, he stares at his hands, simply stares at them, as if he were at the controls of a machine that had broken down. At that moment the mud man walks into the house after fertilizing the lawn.

He wipes off his feet on the rug in the foyer and leaves some grassy deposit in its fibers. He moves toward Thomas with a noise like whispering. Without hesitation he grabs the dragon and the screwdriver and proceeds to pluck out the old batteries and replace them with new ones. And then he continues on to another room of the house to complete some other task and leaves Thomas staring after him.

It is April, and Thomas is busier than ever with so many of his clients rushing to meet the deadline on the fifteenth. Three of them are small-business owners who tried TurboTax and got lost in the paper labyrinth of payroll. They all have ideas about deductions. "But what about . . ." is how most of their sentences begin. They seem to blame him for their mistakes. Secretly he hates them, even as he nods his head and smiles mildly at their jokes about Uncle Sam and says that he will get to work immediately so that they don't have to file for an extension even as he wonders how he will ever find the time.

His wife comes home with a new perfume. Something by Estée Lauder. She leans against Thomas and asks what he thinks. He sniffs at her tentatively. "You smell like flowers," he says. "You smell nice." And then his nose feels suddenly full of ants that needle and burrow and gather into a tremendous sneeze. He moves away from her, bothered by another sneeze, and then another. His eyes water. His upper lip is damp with mucus. His wife asks if he needs a tissue, and he holds out an arm to shoo her away.

The mud man waits in the nearby hallway. He has stopped his sweeping. His hands grip the broom's handle as if it were a sword.

He is looking at Rebecca with his hollowed-out eyes. His nostrils appear to flare. Right then a worm slides its pink head from his forehead, probing the air, pulsing like a hungry vein.

For Easter dinner, the mud man prepares mashed potatoes, a fruit salad, wheat rolls, and a lamb roast jeweled with garlic and rosemary from the garden. The table is set with the wedding china. Two pale green candles sputter against the breeze that purls through an open window. Everyone—even little Owen—makes an *ooo* sound when the mud man carries in the roast on a silver platter and sets it on the table. When he lifts the carving knife, Thomas stands up from his chair so suddenly that it nearly tips over. "I'll take that," he says, and snatches the knife and begins to carve thick, red slices onto plates. He's not sure what's overtaken him, but he suddenly feels annoyed by the mud man, even jealous and proprietary. "There you go," he says, serving the lamb. "There you go."

The mud man watches all of this, as if waiting for an explanation.

Thomas takes his seat at the head of the table. He tucks a napkin under his chin. He looks pointedly at the mud man—and then at his little family—and smiles and says, "Now, doesn't this look delicious."

There is a streetlamp outside his bedroom window. Even on a moonless night, even with the blinds closed, the room glows with a pale blue light. The mud man is backlit by it, a dark silhouette that Thomas observes when he wakes from a nightmare about an audit shutting down his firm.

"Is that you?" Thomas asks, his voice only a whisper. "What do you want?"

The mud man does not say anything. He never says anything. The window is open to let in the cool spring air, and at that moment the wind shifts and sucks the blinds against it with a clatter. The room grows momentarily darker. "Leave me be," Thomas says. "I don't need you right now. Go. Go away."

Thomas comes home to find the stereo blasting. He claps his hands over his ears and says, "What on earth." It's one of his wife's CDs. The Rolling Stones. She loves classic rock, but it gives him an immediate headache and makes his thoughts scatter and his posture stiffen.

In the living room the mud man is dancing. He is bending his knees and pumping his arms. Next to him, Owen leaps about, clapping off-rhythm, and singing, "Yeah, yeah, yeah!" And there is his wife, her hands above her head, twirling in a circle. Her eyes are closed and the corners of her mouth are turned up in a faint smile.

Thomas goes to the stereo and snaps it off and they all go still and he fills the silence by saying, "That's enough of that."

At work, he tells a farmer no, he cannot write off his dog and all of its food and chew toys, even though it chases down mice and nips at the heels of the heifers to hurry them into the barn. At work, he lays out differences between state taxes in Oregon, Washington, Idaho, California, and Wyoming, and makes clear to a musician why he has to file with all of them for the gigs he's played. At work, he tries to explain itemized deductions to a college kid wearing mirrored sunglasses that reflect a warped and ghostly image of himself, his office.

All of them stare at him openmouthed, still pale from winter, bored and confused and annoyed. It's a familiar sensation. He believes he has the same effect on his family.

He comes home to find the house empty. He calls out for his wife, but there is no response. He goes to the bedroom to pull off his tie and change from his suit. There he finds the bed tangled and muddy. He walks toward it slowly, his loafers scuffing the hardwood. He bunches the sheets in his hand and pulls them to his face and breathes deeply. They smell like grass, stone, rain, earthworms.

He feels suddenly boneless, filleted. Dizziness comes over him and he holds out his arms like a man about to fall through rotten ice and catches his weight against the dresser. It is then that his glance falls to the window and he spies them, his wife and the mud man. They are kneeling in the garden, among his daffodils, yanking up weeds to set in piles they will later dispose of. He can hear music faintly through the glass, playing from a boom box they dragged outside. His wife is bobbing her head. Owen plays nearby, pushing a toy truck through his sandbox, his lips pursed, no doubt making little motor sounds. Above them the sky is a lush blue scattered with clouds. The window is latticed and Thomas feels suddenly jailed by it, so separate from them.

All of this is difficult to process, completely outside the boundaries of mathematical principles. He cannot lick his thumb and leaf through a CCH publication or download a PDF from some .gov Web site for the answer. He cannot punch numbers into his calculator and thumb more lead into his mechanical pencil and correct his mistakes with an eraser's grayish-pink nub.

Because he doesn't know what else to do, he slams down his bandaged hand on the dresser. A shock of pain forks up his arm and he relishes its distracting force. With a whimper he slams his hand down again and again until he can feel the heat of blood leaking from him. A perfume bottle rattles and tips and rolls off the dresser to fall to the floor, where it shatters. Its floral scent fogs and spoils the air.

Outside, the mud man turns and raises his head, as though he hears—or maybe senses—Thomas at the window. Across the twenty yards of lawn a stare hardens between them. Thomas tries to hold it, but the perfume makes him sneeze, once, twice. His eyes are watering, tears spilling down his cheeks, so his vision is inexact, but he is almost certain he sees the mud man's normally slack expression tighten into a frown, as if Thomas were a bothersome scrap of dream or maybe a weed that might be unrooted, disposed of, as if he never belonged here in the first place.

Writs of Possession

1.

When Sammy knocks, when she says, "Sheriff's office," she stands to the side of the apartment door. No one has tried to shoot her, not yet. But you never know. The peephole darkens. She waits for the door to rattle open, and when it doesn't, she knocks again. "I know you're in there," she says, and the apartment manager, a man with bony arms and shoe-polish-black hair, leans close to her and says, "He's in there."

This is the Riverside Apartment Complex, and Sammy is a deputy with the Civil Division of the Deschutes County Sheriff's Office. Every day people are falling behind—every day there is a taller stack of evictions, small-claims notices, repossessions of property, wage garnishments for unpaid debts—and every day there is another address to visit, a door to knock on, sometimes to kick down.

The carpet is a burnt orange. The walls are pine paneled. The fluorescent light above them buzzes on and off. She hates her job, hates that she spends most of her day trudging through dumps like this to deliver subpoenas, hurrying people out their doors and down staircases with garbage bags full of clothes, cardboard boxes spilling over with frozen food. In the three years she has worked in the civil division, only once has someone been happy to see her—and she was serving him divorce papers. She seized her baton as he hugged her.

She knocks again, this time using the side of her fist, booming on the door. "Okay," a man's voice says. "I'm opening."

She supposes she feels bad for people when they cry or beg or point to their grubby children and say, "You're doing this to them." Maybe she pities them—that's a better way of putting it. But then a dog will come padding out of a back room or she'll spot a video game console, a pool table, a cappuccino machine. And she'll decide that they're careless and stupid and getting what they deserve. She'll want to say, How much you spend on dog food a month? or How much you think you could've sold that Xbox for? But she won't. Instead, when people show their teeth or kick over chairs or get down on their knees and take her hand and beg, she simply says, "I'm no judge, no jury," so that people contain their anger and sadness, bottle it up for someone else.

Every one of these addresses is like a hole—the same hole, many chambered—and sometimes, when she thinks back on all the homes she's visited, she feels as though she is falling through them, through their living rooms and kitchens, seeing hundreds, thousands of faces all creased and begging, "Don't do this. You don't have to do this."

At her hip she carries handcuffs, a telescoping baton, a .40 caliber Glock. Seven years ago, when she was working patrol, a drunk yanked her ponytail and grated her cheek against the asphalt, and ever since then she's kept her hair cut short. She knows the combination of this and her square face and her wide stance makes her look a little like a man. People blink a few times when they first meet her, trying to make sense of her.

That's the case now, when the door clicks open and she moves into the dim light of the apartment and faces an old man, mid-seventies, wearing pale blue jeans and a ribbed white tank top. His head is bald except for a horseshoe of white hair. His feet are bare—their skin spotted and knotted with veins, the toenails a chalky yellow.

"Milton Ridgeway?"

"Yeah." His square-framed glasses take up most of his face. He peers at her through them and they are thick enough that she can't distinguish the color of his eyes.

"I have a court order," she says and holds out the paper, folded twice as if to better contain the secret. "Notice of eviction."

She steels herself, ready for him to plead his case—like all the others—to smack his fist into an open palm and shout so loudly spittle flies from his lips. To say that he has rights, that this is an illegal eviction. To say that he's been cheated, that the landlord has been cashing his checks all along.

But he doesn't. "Okay," he says and waves both hands as if to clear a bad smell from the air. "Okay. All right."

They are standing in his kitchen. The counter is bare except for a brown mug and a plate dirtied with crumbs. The smell of old coffee and cigarette smoke. Beyond the kitchen, the living room. Same pine-paneled walls and orange carpeting as the hallway. Dirty light seeping in through the tan curtains. A wooden box of a television playing Fox News with the sound off. She wonders if he has children, even grandchildren, who could help. She doesn't see any photos magneted to the fridge, hanging on the walls. Everything is bare.

Milton still hasn't taken the paper. She shakes it at him and he snatches it from her and says, "Fine." He unfolds it and folds it up again without reading, drops it on the counter. "I suppose you want me to leave?"

"Now."

"How long do I have?"

"Now."

"Fine." He walks toward a blackened doorway that must lead to his bedroom, where he pauses. "While you wait, you might want a glass of water? Or some milk?"

No one has ever asked her this before, so it takes her a moment to reply: "No. Thank you."

"I'll only be a minute." He coughs with a sound like pennies rattling at the bottom of a paper cup. "I got to warn you, though. I die sometimes. I been dying all day."

"Excuse me?"

He taps his chest. "My heart stops beating. My lungs stop breathing. I die. Not officially but it's death all the same. Then I wake up. I'm telling you this because I feel a spell coming on. Wouldn't want to alarm you." His smile is damp and pink—he hasn't put in his teeth yet—but she doesn't sense a joke.

She looks to the manager for help, but he is in the hall, muttering into his cell phone. "What should I do?" she says to Milton. "If you die? Do you want me to call an ambulance?"

"Don't do nothing. Give me a couple minutes—I'll come back." He picks at a splinter in the doorframe. "Doctor calls it a heart condition. I call it a Korean condition." His chest hair is as white as dandelion fluff. He reaches into it, under his tank top, and withdraws his dog tags with a tinkle and chime.

Normally she doesn't talk to tenants during repos or evictions except to say, "Hurry," or "I don't care." But Milton is old. And alone. Though she is used to dealing with people who have made the wrong choices, they are, almost all of them, young and furious and seemingly capable of rectifying whatever ruin has come to them. He is different. A lone cloud coming apart in gray filaments, a few drops of rain. She feels, no other word for it, sad.

She calls to him, "Milton?" just as he clicks on the light in his room. His eyes are thin black slits behind his glasses. "You don't mind me asking, what does it feel like? When you die?"

He considers this a moment before answering. "You feel like you're falling," he says. "You feel like you're falling into a very deep hole." His hand makes a downward motion. "Every time I keep expecting to hit bottom. But so far, no bottom."

2.

David peels up the duck-patterned linoleum in the bathroom and lays down tile. He rips away the aquamarine carpet in the guest room and pries out the hundreds of tacks and staples beneath it to reveal the hardwood beneath. He scores the floral wallpaper in the kitchen and sprays it with DIF and scrapes it off in damp shreds and gouges the drywall so that he must mud and texture before splashing the walls over with paint. He unscrews the light fixtures—all white orbs with brass collars—and replaces them with wrought iron. He hangs new gutters. He trades out the appliances for stainless steel. He installs new hardware on all the cabinets. He removes the cracked and yellowed switches and outlets and screws in white plates.

Now the house looks like the house he imagined when, five years ago, he walked through it and laid his hands on its walls and said, "I can see the potential." Five years and he hasn't flipped open his toolbox until now—now that he has to move. His marriage is falling apart. His daughter is starting to bring home college brochures. His boss at the biodiesel company ordered a thirty-day furlough for all employees. So he spends his evenings and weekends alone; his wife has moved in with her parents and his daughter spends all her time in her room. All of his time is devoted to restoring a house he has come to hate, to think of as a kind of grave, for someone else to enjoy.

The back porch overlooks a hillside crowded with big pines. For the decorative posts—staggered every ten feet along the railing, squared and beveled, as tall as a rifle and as thick as a thigh—the builder didn't use the treated fir or cedar he should have, and dry rot set in. When David pulls off the old sheathing, tearing into it with a hammer and a short crowbar, he reveals their hollow core, and in it, the skeletons of four birds along with their rotten wig of a nest.

David uses the crowbar to claw them from the post, their tomb. Bones and branches and broken bits of shell scatter at his feet. He toes at a skull and it crumbles into a white powder. He guesses the birds were nesting when the house was being framed, maybe up in the rafters, and the builder climbed a ladder and cradled the nest in his hands and cooed and whistled at the baby birds and then tossed them inside the post before hammering on its cap and whispering good-bye.

3.

For more than a month they have lived here. A month is the longest they have ever gone before getting caught—the owners walking in on them watching television, taking a shower, knifing mustard across bread. Then they run—they have learned to be fast—and eventually find another house.

They look for a subdivision with brickwork driveways and three-car garages, with columns flanking the front doors and maple saplings struggling to grow in the front yards. They find a three- or four-story house with no dog toys or playground equipment in its backyard. They discover an unlocked window or a sliding glass door. In a guest room in the far corner of the walkout basement, they drop their backpacks. They wait.

The first few days, they spend a lot of time listening to the footsteps thumping overhead, the muttered conversations overheard through the heating ducts and thinly insulated walls. They take note of the owners' patterns. If there are no children and no pets, it usually means the couple spend their days, sometimes their nights, working, these doctors and lawyers and engineers. What little time they do spend at home, they spend in their room watching Netflix.

After the shower creaks off, after the dishes clink in the sink, after the door slams and the Lexus growls to life and the garage door rumbles closed, the house is empty and will typically remain so until evening comes.

So the two of them—the boy and the girl, brother and sister, homeless for more than two years after running away several times from foster care—they steal the clothes from the edges of the closet, the backs of drawers. They pawn the jewelry and cameras and DVDs. They slip money—just a few bills, not enough for anyone to notice unless they were really looking—from wallets and purses. They walk on the sides of their feet so that they don't leave tracks in the white carpet. They hide from the maid when she comes, on Mondays and Thursdays. But mostly they just hang out, watch television, raid the fridge for treats.

One morning, they are in a master bedroom with a vaulted ceiling, a four-poster king-size bed, and two walk-in closets, each of them bigger than any bedroom they've ever called their own. An archway leads into the bathroom, where the toilet rises up on a pedestal and the counters are marble and the shower is surrounded by glass bricks and the tub is a deep cauldron with two dozen jets.

The sister rummages through the closet and climbs into a suit seven sizes too big, while the brother pulls on a black cocktail dress that won't zip up his broad back. A flat-screen television hangs on the wall. They punch through the channels, finally settling on VH1—a best of the eighties countdown—and leap from one side of the bed to the other, playing air guitar, yowling along with the hair bands.

They are laughing, hitting each other with pillows, when the screen goes dark and the music silences. They stand in a mess of sheets, breathing heavily. A man is watching them. His face is a severe shade of red. He has small eyes and a pinched mouth. He is as tall as a doorway. They recognize him from the photo albums shelved in the living room and the wedding photo hanging in the hallway.

The brother and sister look at each other—neither of them knowing what to do. He is blocking the door. And the nearest window drops twenty feet into a thorny hedge, a broken leg.

"Who are you," the man says, not yelling, not yet, "and what are you doing in my house?"

In another story, they might have told him their names. They might have told him about their father running off, their mother drinking heavily—the social workers with their tired eyes and sleepy-sounding voices, the cat piss–stinking foster homes decorated with crosses and strangely colored paintings of Jesus petting sheep. And the man might have listened. His eyes might have softened. His posture might have relaxed. He might even have smiled briefly when they told him about the week they spent living in a Walmart.

And when they finally said, We're sorry. We'll leave now, he would have shouted, No!, his arms outstretched to block their way. No, he would say, his voice softer this time. Stay. Please. And the brother and sister would shrug at each other when he motioned them downstairs, when he led them to the kitchen, where they would make turkey sandwiches and pour tall glasses of milk and eat together in the nook that overlooked the green expanse of lawn that ran into a pond with a concrete swan spitting an arc of water in the middle of it.

When they were finished eating their sandwiches, when they had licked their lips and settled back in their chairs, he would look out the window and quietly ask if they would like to stay. They would say no, they couldn't, they had to move on, and he would say, Stay, really, I mean it—and they would know that he meant it, that he wasn't going to trick them and call the police, that maybe the house felt a little too big for him, that maybe he needed them as much as they needed him, and they would all smile as they finished their glasses of milk.

But that is another story.

4.

There is a knock at the door. At first Paul doesn't hear it because of the TV—the game show that doesn't require talent, only luck, the contestants choosing among the fifty beautiful women who stand onstage holding silver briefcases full of money. Paul is yelling when he first hears the knock, throwing up his arms and condemning the greed of the man who could have gone home with a hundred grand but decided to keep playing. "The idiocy," Paul says. "The fucking idiocy people are capable of."

The knock sounds again and Paul mutes the volume and goes to the door, wondering vaguely who it might be, maybe the Jehovah's Witnesses he saw prowling the neighborhood earlier? Or Papa John's? Had he ordered a pizza? He had, hadn't he? It is so hard to remember anything anymore, every day bleeding into the next, a weekday the same as a weekend, night no different from day, ever since he lost his job.

Two men stand in the yellow cone of his porch light. They wear black boots and black jeans and black T-shirts. Their hair is buzzed. Their shoulders are humped with muscle. Behind them stands a cop—black windbreaker with a yellow star on the breast. A woman, he realizes, only when she speaks, when she hands him a piece of paper. A repossession notice, she explains.

He looks at the paper, but doesn't really read it. The men shoulder their way past Paul, while the woman tells him they are here to re-trieve the fifty-five-inch HD plasma he bought on an installment plan at Best Buy. He was one thousand dollars into his three-thousand-dollar payment plan when he lost his job as a financial consultant at Wells Fargo. He has not, as he has advised so many others to do, nested away his money. For the first three months he lived off his sev-erance pay. He sent out queries for jobs that did not exist. He has not applied for unemployment. He has not asked his parents for help, has not even told them he lost his job. He has not written a check in six months, doesn't answer the phone when the creditors call, will not listen to the messages that go from stern to condemning.

The woman remains on the porch as the men approach Paul's television, which rests on a two-tiered glass console with black metal legs. One of them hits the power button and shoves the re-mote in his pocket. Then they rip the wires from the wall and wrap them around their fists. They station themselves at either side of the television and say, "Ready?" and lift it without any trouble. It ought to weigh more, Paul thinks, considering how much it cost. He is folding the repossession paper in half and then in half again, and then again, making a tiny square he can close his fist around. He does not feel much of anything. These past few days he has spent mostly on the couch, his mind empty except for simple needs, the next diet soda he will drink, the next program he will watch.

Their invasion of his condo does not bother him, not particularly, even though they act like the television is theirs, like their employer is a parent and they are its vengeful children. He is too tired to care. It isn't until one of the men bumps into him and says, "Move, loser," that something sparks inside him, something electric, as he remembers the weight of his manager's hand on his shoulder—the sad smiles of his coworkers when, in a daze, he packed up his desk—the Walmart bag he found on his front porch the next day, full of the things he left behind, his Trail Blazers coffee mug, his calculator from college, the M. C. Escher calendar.

On the coffee table sits a half-empty bottle of Budweiser. The glass is warm in his hand when he picks it up. The men are not looking at him. They are looking at the open doorway, taking baby steps toward it, taking care not to trip over a magazine rack, to knock against the edge of the coffee table. And the cop is already gone, walking toward the black sedan parked in the street.

Paul doesn't say anything when he approaches the men, doesn't release the scream he feels building inside him. He simply snaps his arm—and sends the bottle spiraling through the air and into the gray eye of the television, shattering it.

5.

Mr. Peterson has taken a job in Seattle with a software company. As part of the hiring bonus, if the house doesn't sell within the next two months, the company will offer him x amount of money and assume the title.

The Petersons try. Some of the neighbors will admit to that—they do try. They install new countertops, new carpeting, new sinks and faucets. They brush paint on the walls. They remove all of their family photos and hide all of their toys so that the house could belong to anyone, so that the couples who follow high-heeled, lipsticked real-estate agent through the rooms, up and down the stairs, their fingers lingering on the railings and doorknobs, can imagine the house as their own.

They list the home for $599,000—a fair price, everyone agrees. A price that will reflect well on the neighborhood. But the months pass without an offer. And the Petersons' garage fills steadily with cardboard boxes sealed with tape. And then one day the Bekins trucks pull up to the curb and the movers—the sweating, thick-waisted men with goatees—leap out to haul away all of the furniture and books and wedding china. They leave the house vacant of everything except the window treatments and the dimples the couches crushed into the carpet.

Now the original real-estate sign comes down and another one goes up listing the house at $399,000. The neighborhood, red-faced and narrow-eyed, hates the Petersons for this. Over the past few years they have watched property values climb—doubling, tripling—and they have counted on that equity. They believe in their houses as investments more than as places to live. So they scowl at the empty house as if it is to blame. They call the agent—they call the Petersons—to express their outrage. They encourage their dogs—their yellow Labs and golden retrievers and Siberian huskies—to shit in the front yard. Someone spray-paints *FUCK YOU* in big black letters across the garage door, but the next day it is painted over. Someone rips the real-estate sign from the front yard and shoves it into a nearby storm drain, but the next day it is up again—and within a week it is topped by a red banner that reads *sale pending*.

In this neighborhood, a subdivision called Swan Hollow, no one can paint their houses anything but earth tones. Nor can they plant vegetables or store play equipment in their front yards. They cannot park RVs and boats in their driveways for more than twenty-four hours. And when you live in a neighborhood like this, there are certain expectations of you. There are rules you must abide by, and now the rules have been broken.

So they wait until it is night. The streetlamps buzz to life. The garage doors roll open. People collect red three-gallon jugs of gasoline and carry them sloshing down the block and gather in the driveway of the house, the empty house. There are twenty people altogether, mostly members of the neighborhood association. Others watch from their front porches. The moon is out, and its reflection glows in the living room window like a spectral eye. The siding is vinyl and the porch boards are made of recycled plastic and nobody knows how well these will burn. They want inside— they want the house to burn from the belly up.

They try to kick open the front door, but it is dead bolted and no one can make it splinter inward like on the cop shows on TV. So they circle the house and try the windows and find one of them unlocked and rip off the screen and boost a middle-aged woman named Susan Pearl through it so that she can unlock the front door and allow them to rush inside, to splash gasoline along the walls, to soak pools of it into the carpet and waterfall it down the stairs. Their eyes tear over. The fumes make them dizzy. They cough and laugh at once.

They make a trail of gasoline—gasoline they would have otherwise used to power their riding lawn mowers across lawns of Kentucky bluegrass—they make a trail of gasoline down the porch, along the pebbled path, to the driveway, where Susan sparks her pink rhinestone Zippo and lights a menthol cigarette and takes a deep drag off it and flicks it in a sparking arc.

Her lipstick has made a red collar around the filter that matches the red ember at its tip. It spins through the air and bounces off the cement and comes to a stop in a pool of gas that ignites with a huff. A tongue of blue-and-orange flame licks its way speedily toward the house.

It isn't long before the windows explode and the flames rise through them and the siding around them blackens and buckles and melts and runs like tears. Sparks swirl up into the night, lost among the stars. The roof is replaced by a crown of flame. The street appears sunlit. The heat is tremendous. Everyone staggers out of the driveway, into the street, the shadows playing across their faces making them appear as strangers to one another.

6.

Tonight the mother reads the little boy the story *Harold and the Purple Crayon*. They lay side by side in his bed, and when she finishes, when she snaps shut the book, he asks her to stay a little longer. "To cuddle, Mama." She tells him no. She has to go. He has to sleep. "Just for a minute," he says. "A mini-minute," she says and remains curled up by him for a few breaths before climbing out of bed and pulling the covers up to his chin. "Don't leave," he says and she says she has to and kisses his forehead and lets her lips linger there another moment before she snaps off the light, says goodnight, closes the door.

He's not scared of the dark. He's not worried about monsters beneath his bed or aliens at the window. It's his mother—whose eyes are red-rimmed, whose hair is going gray at the roots because she hasn't been to the beauty parlor in months—who worries him. He hears her crying through the walls. He hears her on the phone: "We're underwater," she keeps saying, along with that word, *foreclosure*. They are going into foreclosure.

One night he asked her where it was, foreclosure. "I'm sorry?" she said and he said, "You keep saying we're going there. Foreclosure." Her lips flattened and her eyebrows came together and she asked him if he wanted to watch cartoons—would he like that?

He has heard at Sunday school the story of Noah and the ark that survived the great flood. And he has seen on the news the waters that rose up from a river to swallow towns in a place called Iowa. This is what his mother is worried about, he feels certain. This is why she is packing all of their things into boxes, suitcases. A flood is coming. And its waters will be black and roiling with terrible fish, their eyes white, their fangs thin and crooked. He imagines the first wave of the flood surging along the street, splashing against the side of their house, foaming and reeking of the fish that wait outside, gnawing at the wood. The water will seep under the doors and burble its way down the hallway, rising, rising.

He needs to work quickly. And he knows his mother might notice the light under his door, so he pulls the shades instead, allowing the moon into his room, its light silvering his walls. Slowly he slides open his closet. From a shelf devoted to art supplies he pulls a box of crayons and fumbles through them until he chooses the one he thinks to be purple, though it could just as well be black in the uncertain moonlight.

And there, on the wall, he begins to draw a boat, one big enough for the two of them, to carry them away to foreclosure.

7.

Her hearing isn't what it used to be, but Gertie can still hear the knock at the door, even from upstairs. She doesn't like to be bothered, likes to keep to herself. When the phone rings, she lets the answering machine pick up. And at church—her only destination these days besides the doctor's office—the First Baptist Church, where she serves as a deaconess, where she has hardly missed a Sunday in fifty years, she shakes hands during the sharing of the peace and lingers afterward for coffee, but doesn't go out of her way to say much except "Lovely day," or "Lovely to see you." So when she hears the knock at the door, she goes to the window of her bedroom, pulls aside the lace curtain, peers down at the front porch.

Nobody knows about her troubles. Nobody asks how she is getting along, and even if they did, she likely wouldn't tell them. She has never been one to complain. Not about the arthritis chewing at her fingers and not about the cataract that fogs over her left eye and not about how badly she misses Harry, how empty the house feels without him. And not about the crooks—though she'd like to give them an earful, maybe crack them over the head with a can of soup—who convinced her to take out a thirty-year, 6.4 percent mortgage for thirty seven thousand dollars, along with a ten-thousand-dollar line of credit.

She and her husband have owned the home since 1951, raised their son here, his height still faintly sketched in the kitchen cupboard door, the pencil marks the same gray as the broken blood vessels that trail down her legs. She couldn't keep up with the payments. Over and over the writs of possession have been posted on her door. Over and over she has ripped them down and placed them at the bottom of her garbage can, as if the dark truth contained in them might decompose along with the coffee grounds, dissolve like a communion wafer on her tongue and absolve her.

On the porch stands the policeman—no, a woman, Gertie realizes, when the figure moves into a slant of sunlight—peering into the living room through the bay window, a big woman with the haircut and bowlegged stance of a man. She knows Gertie is home—her Buick is parked in the driveway. The policewoman isn't going away this time. She isn't going to post another notice and clomp down the porch and zip away in her unmarked car. She hammers at the door again and then tries the knob, so that Gertie imagines she can feel the force of the hand on her, shaking her, strangling her.

Gertie withdraws from the window and the lace curtain falls gently into place like a spiderweb. Her husband is dead. Her son is dead too. So many of her friends and neighbors. Everyone is dead. She says this out loud—"Everyone is dead"—her voice a metallic rasp as she pulls open the drawer of the night table and pulls out the revolver, the .357 her husband kept around the house for security. It is heavy—she holds it in a two-handed grip, the muzzle drooping, aimed at the floor between her legs. She sits on the edge of the bed.

The springs moan. The policewoman hammers at the door again—and then yells something, Gertie doesn't know what.

She can't recall if Harry ever took the gun to the shooting range or out to a gravel pit to blast pop bottles. As far as she knows, it has never been fired. She wonders vaguely how old the bullets are, whether they can expire, when she brings the muzzle to her breast—not her mouth, that would be too much trouble to clean up, too much ugliness to look at for whoever found her—and pulls the trigger.

8.

The neighborhood is empty. It has always been empty. It was built by a custom-home builder that has developed subdivisions in three different states. Since the market crashed, the company has laid off most of its employees in its building and land development divisions. It is working with financial advisers and legal counsel on vendor payments and other cash obligations.

Construction has stopped. All the signs and sales trailers have been hauled away. No sod has been laid; the yards are made of mud. The farther you travel into the neighborhood, the more unfinished it becomes. Some houses are missing windows and doors. Some houses are naked, without siding, and the sheets of felt paper stapled to their exterior come loose and flap in the wind like rotten skin. Some houses are nothing more than a skeletal frame and some lots are nothing more than an excavated hole, a muddy cavity collapsing inward.

The neighborhood backs up against a pine forest. And it isn't long—after the payloaders and bulldozers and trucks stacked high with lumber drive away—before the animals begin to creep from the shadows, to explore the houses and consider them a kind of nest or burrow.

A barred owl sails into an attic—through the octagonal hole cut for a gable vent—and makes it his roost. Crows blacken the rafters of an unfinished frame. A bear claws open a garden shed and roots into its bare floor. Feral cats wander the streets. Wasps and swallows mud over the eaves.

Beyond the subdivision's pillared entryway—Eagle Ridge, reads the gold lettering with etched cattails rising around it—stands a model home, a design known as the Apex IV. Four thousand square feet of hardwood flooring and enameled woodwork, formal and informal dining rooms, study, great room, and a kitchen bigger than most restaurants', with quartz countertops, a center island, and custom maple cabinetry throughout.

Months ago, a real-estate agent left the back door unlocked, and tonight it comes unstuck when a hard wind sucks it open. It chirps and swings on its hinges, as though beckoning the forest. And the forest answers. From between its trees steals a pack of coyotes that noses through the door and into the kitchen, where they sniff the air. No one has been here for a long time: the house is theirs. They yip and whine and set off through the many rooms. Their paws whisper across the carpet, and their claws click the tiles and hardwood. They pee in the corners. They gnaw at the legs of the dining room table. They leap onto the beds and leather couches and snap playfully at one another.

One day a teenager in a Ramones T-shirt with nothing better to do hurls a brick through the Apex IV's picture window. It shatters inward, a gaping hole framed by fangs of glass. The teenager holds up his fists, charged up with music of destruction, the crash and tinkle of broken glass still biting the air soon replaced by snarls and yaps that come from inside the house and that merge into a terrible howling, the howling of a dozen coyotes, growing louder and louder. The teenager drops his hands. The smile on his face fades. He stumbles back, into the street, where his bike lies on its side.

He climbs onto it and kicks at the pedals to get them turning, to get the bike moving, just as the pack of coyotes pours through the broken window, a heaving gray wave of them, all jabbering and clacking their teeth as they pursue him for his trespass.

9.

Sammy can't dwell on the sad stories. The family that moved into their van. The man who says his store has been empty ever since the second Walmart opened up. The woman who says her husband has cancer, says their insurance dropped them, says they had to put all their medical expenses on their credit cards. The sour piles of laundry in the corners, the stained pizza boxes and crumpled soda cans decorating the floor, the child wearing a T-shirt as a dress, clutching a one-armed teddy bear.

Sometimes she wishes she lived in a world without doors. There's too much hurt out there, and every time she opens a door, she opens herself to it, their collected voices, their collected failure—all powered by voices that scream and whine and blame and beg and reason—punctuated now by a gunshot on a summer afternoon.

She should cry out, Sheriff's office! and kick the door until it splinters from its hinges. She should pound up the stairs. She should check one room after another until she finds the red stain on the wall. She should lean over the body and check for a pulse. Maybe, for once, she can help. Maybe she can actually do some good.

But this is a door Sammy can't bring herself to open. There is a body waiting for her inside and she can't face it. Because that would feel too much like murder.

She drops the eviction notice and it flutters to the porch and she stares at it for a long time before stepping out of the house's shadow and into the sun. She heads back to the car, where she will radio an ambulance before cruising off to the next neighborhood, the next address, the next door to bang her knuckles on, dreading what waits for her.

The Balloon

The sickness begins with a cough, a needling itch at the back of your throat that grows worse until it feels like your lungs are sleeved with burrowing ants that you must expel, barking raggedly into your hands until they are spotted with blood. Accompanying this is a fever so powerful that a wet washcloth steams when placed on your forehead. Your brain cooks. Your vision twirls red. And all this time you are coughing, coughing, until it feels as though your guts might uproot and push out your throat.

Among the people of River Falls, Oregon, its first victim is Geoff Meyer, a roofer with tarry fingers, a bowed back, and a loping gait from all his time spent cobbling shingles together, clambering across gables and hips and valleys. One day, he comes home from work hacking into his fist, and when his wife asks him if he is all right, he nods through his coughing and pushes past her to the bathroom, where he runs a hot shower and curls up at the bottom of the tub, hoping the steam will help. But his chest continues to convulse, his throat continues to scream, and eventually his wife comes to check on him, and by that time the water has gone cold and she is in a panic, shaking him, taking in big gulps of the air he has infected, calling out, "Sara, Sara—come—you've got to come."

Sara, their daughter, is densely built—mostly torso, with tiny, delicate feet. When she goes out to eat, she orders chicken fingers, Philly cheesesteak sandwiches, iceberg lettuce salads drenched in Western dressing. She is in her thirties but still lives with her parents in a room that had not changed much since she was in high school: the same posters, the same stained purple carpet, the same fantasy novels lining her bookshelves, the same white wicker hamper overflowing with sweatshirts and jeans, the same comforter with a shaggy-maned unicorn on it.

She has a four-poster bed and to each post she ties a balloon. She has been doing this ever since she received the bed as a gift, on her sixteenth birthday. When she climbs under the covers every night, she likes to imagine she is floating away, out the window, into the night sky, above the moonlit table of clouds, where dreams wait for her. She refreshes the balloons every week, when they begin to wilt. Her desk, situated beneath the window, was her mother's old sewing table. She rests her feet on the ironwork pedal when she sits there and scribbles in composition booklets, crafting stories about princesses—not the kind who fall asleep from cursed spindles or poisoned apples, but the kind with golden armor and a sword called Oathmaker that can slay dragons and lop off troll heads with a single swing. She writes so often that the desktop carries the design of a half-formed triangle from the oils of her arms. People often say to her, "Sara? You there?," and when she smiles and nods, they say, "For a second, you seemed to be someplace else."

She works as a receptionist at Greeley Chiropractic—answering phones through a headset, greeting every patient by name, arranging the magazines in the shape of a fan on the glass-topped table in the waiting area, refilling the triangular-paper-cup dispenser for the water cooler that burps every time someone gets a drink—until her father and then her mother fall ill, and she takes her vacation time to nurse them. She brews tea, helps them back and forth to the bathroom, packs bags of ice into their armpits and elbows, around their necks, over their wrists, and then refills the bags when they melt into warm-bellied jellyfish that slosh and roll off her parents' bodies when a coughing fit seizes them.

Sara goes to Walgreens to buy cough syrup and cough drops and ibuprofen and cold packs. She goes to Food 4 Less to buy chicken soup, chamomile tea. She goes to the gas station to fill up her hatchback. She has not washed her hands. Her fingers are sticky with the spit and sweat of her parents. Everywhere she goes, so does the infection, on the cart with the wobbly wheel she pushes, the apples she fondles and then replaces in their bin, the twenty-dollar bill she pulls from her purse, the counter she taps as she waits for her receipt.

It isn't long before the hospitals are full, before the schools are closed, before the sidewalks grow crowded with reporters. Three people die. And then, in one night, three hundred. Everyone rushes the grocery stores and pulls off the shelves cereals, pastas, granola bars, canned fruits and vegetables, bottled water, whatever will last even after the electricity snaps off. The worst is happening, they are saying. The worst is here.

When parents say, "You'll catch your death," they mean it, grabbing their children as they race out the door to hand them a jacket, yes, but also a surgical mask. "Stay in the yard," they say. Don't breathe, they want to say.

Sara imagines the sickness as the fluffy spores that float off a dandelion—or the cloth-winged moths that swarm the lamps in the Walmart parking lot—and she keeps her eyes sharp on the air around her as if she could see the sickness coming, maybe dodge it. This is October and the leaves on the aspen and the cottonwoods turn a shimmering gold and come loose from their branches. You can see the shape of the wind in them, the leaves that wend and eddy in the streets, lawns, ballparks, making a skittering, clattery music, like skeletons softly dancing.

Everyone buys masks. Not just surgical masks—because the

stores go empty of them almost immediately—but carpenters' masks, gas masks, even Halloween masks. Anything to choke away the germs.

Hank Haines is balding. What little hair he has left is a frizzy black halo. His thighs rub together when he walks and he can fit his fist into his belly button. He works as a deputy sheriff in Deschutes County. Most of his days are spent in a rust-speckled squad car parked behind a pine windbreak. He waits for speeders to hurl by as he aims his radar gun out the window and imagines it into a rifle that would take out the tires of a Mustang with ten kilos of black tar heroin in the trunk. His real gun, a Glock 35, he has never actually drawn, though he dreams of doing so every day.

He has always imagined himself a hero. Not for anything he has done, but for what he is capable of doing. When he stands in line at the credit union, he knows exactly how he will react when the robbers in black ski masks rush in and say, Anybody moves and you're dead meat! When children bumble too close to the road, he carefully eyes them and readies to rush out and snatch them from the path of an oncoming semi. He always sits at the back of restaurants, facing the door, ready for the unexpected. His entire life is made up of moments like this, sewed together like a bunch of hypothetical merit badges.

When he was a boy, Hank was constantly afraid. He would run past the graveyard on his way home from school. He would sleep with his desk lamp glowing all night. He would wrap his sheets around him tightly, a blowhole the only part of him exposed. One night, he was so convinced that a pale skinless creature waited for him under his bed, ready to seize his ankle with a long-fingered hand, that he held his bladder until he pissed himself and lay in his bed whimpering until morning, when his mother found him.

He would never tell anybody this, God forbid, but he always felt a little jealous of Rapunzel. Because she was safe. No one could get her and no one expected anything of her. If he was her, he would have cut off all that hair and called it good.

Now the old fears are washing over him again. He sits in his squad car, the windows sealing him in a protective bubble. He imagines the ground rumbling beneath him and knuckling upward into a spire—higher and higher still—until he is balanced two hundred feet in the air. The Crown Vic will become his tower, and there he can wait all of this out. Because people want him to do something, but he doesn't know what.

He watches the cars stream out of River Falls. Occasionally he flashes his lights at speeders, but doesn't pull anyone over, for fear that they are sick. He buys a gas mask from the Army Surplus and wears it at all times except when sleeping. Sometimes, when he hears the radio squawk and the dispatcher call out his name, he wants to snap it off, afraid of what he might be asked to do, ashamed that he hasn't changed at all, that he is still that boy in the piss-soaked frog pajamas.

Hank remembers what his high school counselor once told him—to control his fears he must control his breathing, to imagine the air around him as a humored essence. What was his favorite fruit? Peaches. He loved canned peaches. And what was the color of illness? Green. That's the color people turned in cartoons when they felt sour in the guts, wobbly-kneed. "Good," the counselor told him. "Now imagine those colors moving in and out of your body. Breathe in peach, breathe out green. Peach in, green out." All the ugly feelings will leave him, making room for the good, purifying him. And now, with his gas mask snugly fit around his face, as long as he thinks about his breathing, as long as he controls what goes in and out of him, he is hopeful he is safe. In with the peach, out with the green.

It takes Sara's parents five days to die. During that time, their chests seem to collapse inward with every hitching cough. Their throats rasp. Their lips bruise. The blood vessels in their eyes burst, and they weep blood, and because they are propped up on their pillows, the blood runs down their cheeks in paths that seem raked by claws. The doctor prescribes medicine, but it does not help. When they die, within hours of each other, their bodies go slack. The sudden silence makes the air feel brittle.

In a kind of trance, Sara stumbles to the kitchen to turn on the radio—for the noise, something to distract her from what has happened—then kills it when the music breaks for an update on the sickness the scientists are now calling H3L1, or Hell, the nickname goes.

A Budweiser delivery truck pulls up to Food 4 Less and an hour later pulls away. A Greyhound grumbles back and forth to Portland, its tailpipe coughing along with its gray-faced passengers. A charter plane. A station wagon. A bicyclist passing through on his way across the state. And all those letters licked shut. The sickness spreads. However many hundred become however many thousand become however many million in a matter of days. There isn't time for quarantine. There is barely enough time to utter the word *pandemic*.

And by then the sickness has extended across the state, the country, the continent, the world. There is no difference between good and bad, young and old, not that the sickness recognizes. Everyone is eligible for death.

For a few days, the world blames River Falls—calling it ground zero—so that the town feels like the eye of a black whirlpool with clotted lungs and broken bones swirling through it. And in turn River Falls blames Sara's family. It feels good to have someone to blame. They gather together on the sidewalks and in the pews of churches, speaking hoarsely to one another, peppermints and cough drops clicking between their teeth. When they talk, they look in the direction of her house, the brick ranch with its shades pulled and its lawn busy with weeds, and they whisper terrible things about the Meyers, damn them for what they've done, and damn Sara for not falling ill like the rest of them—what is she, some kind of witch? Is this the devil's business, then?

Sara keeps waiting for the sickness to take her. She plugs a thermometer into her mouth every hour on the hour. She pays close attention to her throat, waiting for the itching, and every now and then gives a tentative cough just to see what will happen. One afternoon, when she drives to the grocery store to fill her pantry, as the television advises, a half dozen people rush her in the parking lot. They wear masks and they grab her wrists and pull at her clothes.

"Thanks," they say. "Thanks a lot."

"They've run out of coffins? Did you hear that, Sara?"

These are voices she knows—from school, from work, from the neighborhood—voices muffled by masks and soured with venom.

A woman in a bird mask says, "Look at what you've done." This is Maggie Meyerhofer, whose eyes are a startled blue and stare out from holes in her mask.

And then a man, Chuck Wilson, who came into the chiropractor regularly with lower back pain and who always wore flannel shirts even in the height of summer and whose face is now hidden by a zombie mask with an eyeball hanging from its socket, says, "Why aren't you dead? Why aren't you dying?"

His voice is overrun by that of a girl Sara went to high school with, Lauren Stott, who snatches a fistful of Sara's hair to bring her close and whisper harshly, "My boy is dead because of you." Her head is encased in a yellow rubber ball with a smiley face printed across it.

Their mouths are like dark furnaces. The words come between coughs, struggling to be heard.

"I'm sorry," Sara says. She doesn't know what else to say except, "Leave me alone," when a voice yells over all the other voices to say that maybe her blood is an elixir, that maybe if they drink it they will be cured.

She wishes she had her sword, Oathmaker. Not to hurt them. Merely to show them. All she would need to do is slide the blade from its scabbard—and its steel would glow and its keen edge would sing when she swung it one way, then the other. And they would shrink away from her.

Their eyes are sunken. Their skin the gray of rotting fence posts. They cough at her—yes, at her—trying to infect her, despite what they already know, that she can't be infected, that she will outlive them all.

As she rushes back to her car, they chase her and yell after her as if their words are pliers and hammers and duct tape, instruments of torture, tools that might interpret their rage and helplessness.

Hank has spent most of his life waiting for trouble, and now that trouble has found him, he isn't sure quite what to do with it. He drives the streets of town. He spots a corpse on a porch swing, another in the park, a woman splayed out in the shape of an X, as if she has fallen from a building that isn't there. A man runs by carrying a television set. Fire rises from the roof of a two-story Victorian and a column of smoke rises from the fire, hazing into the far reaches of the sky. He drives by all of this and stops only when he sees something manageable, seemingly safe, an old woman lugging a twenty-pound sack of rice. She wears a gray cotton sweat suit and a surgical mask. White hair spills down her shoulders. She takes small shuffling steps, clutching the bag of rice to her chest, leaning backward at the hips to manage the weight.

He pulls up alongside her and says, "Can I give you a ride, ma'am?" His voice sounds hollow and foreign inside the gas mask.

"No," she says without looking at him. The wind rises and leaves shiver.

"Can I help you carry that bag then?"

She turns away from him and cries over her shoulder. "It's mine. Don't touch it."

He is getting out of his car at this point, walking toward her. "You look like you could use some—"

She drops the bag of rice and it hits the cement with a thud. "I said it's mine—it's mine—it's mine!" With the final *mine*, she claws at his outstretched hand and the skin along the back of it comes away in curls like a clumsily peeled apple.

"Ouch! Jesus, lady."

She hoists up the bag of rice and continues to hobble home.

He returns to the squad car and slathers the wound with ointment, then wraps it in gauze from the first aid kit. Peach in, green out—that's what he keeps saying to himself—peach in, green out. He has always taken pride in his ability to act. At least in his mind, which is like a scroll of blank comic panels. He could walk a few steps forward and sketch in a scene where, maybe, he speared to death a tentacled monster or carried in his arms a buxom woman. Somewhere, in a panel in the far distance, he is galloping on a white horse. Or standing on top of a building, silhouetted by the moon, cape flapping.

But now the panels seem torn and pitted and the drawings he imagines upon them are done sloppily in crayon.

His radio is silent. The police station is empty except for a dead man in a holding cell, his cheek glued to a bloody pool of vomit. No one asks Hank to do anything so he doesn't do anything, doesn't protest the looting, doesn't investigate the intermittent gunfire. Instead he drives to his cabin in the woods to hide.

At a time when everyone should stay home—that's what the television says, before the channels give way to static, "Stay home"— people instead go to church. At Saint Cecilia's and at Trinity Lutheran and at the United Methodist, people wander in and out throughout the day. The services and vigils are ongoing. The candles are burned down to bubbling nubs of wax. Everyone wears their masks, but the masks don't help. They breathe one another's breath and they bring their hands together in prayer and they sing, how sweet the sound, until the coughing overwhelms them and they hunch over and fall to their knees in awful genuflection.

Sara's fridge is nearly empty. Her cupboard too. She cuts the moldy rind off a brick of cheddar and eats its untouched heart. She eats the olives her mother used for martinis even though she hates their bitter taste. And then she lies in her bed, the bed with the balloons tied to its four posts, where she always feels safest. When she was eighteen she painted the ceiling a pale blue scattered with fluffy white clouds. She does not imagine it as the sky outside her house, but another sky, another world, where the sun shines and she rules with mercy from a castle with towers fluttering with pennants and walls decorated with the scales of all the dragons she has slain.

The mural gives her such a sense of space, of outward possibility. The balloons will take her there, away.

Dogs roam in packs. They race in and out of abandoned houses, burrowing through the trash and cupboards unmolested, gnawing on the bloated corpses found hunched over dining room tables and floating in bathtubs full of cold, rank water. The dogs sleep on couches and on beds, their bodies piled together, fat and filthy. Their howls fill the night like an air-raid siren. One day, Sara wanders outside, climbing up the porches of her neighbors' houses to ring doorbells, calling out, "Anybody?" Her father was part of a regional softball team and she carries his bat with her, imagining it as her sword, Oathmaker.

There is nothing left in her kitchen now but a half sleeve of rice cakes and few mucky knife swipes of peanut butter in a jar. She does not feel sad. She feels completely blank.

The day is windy. Newspapers flutter. Beer cans rattle. Sara wanders into the park and climbs onto a swing and absently kicks her legs. This is where the dogs find her. There are ten of them. Labradors and boxers and Dobermans and German shepherds, even a goldendoodle. They slink toward her with their ears and tails flattened.

She stands from the swing and snatches up the softball bat and tightens her grip and brings it to her shoulder and says, like a teary prayer, "I am the knight and you are the dragons."

Hank sits on his porch with his Glock in his lap. He is certain someone will come. When he least expects it, when his back is turned, someone will come creeping out of the woods to pry the lock off his door or rip the mask from his face. He startles often at his shadow, his reflection in the mirror, a stranger in a gas mask. To stay awake he chews NoDoz and sucks on coffee beans and drinks cans of warm Mountain Dew. Sometimes he isn't sure whether he is awake or asleep or somewhere in between, the world warping along the edges. He is certain only about sitting still, waiting, and watching for endless hours. This is his tower. He will defend his tower.

His vision of the world is limited to a half acre of meadow, the woods surrounding it, and the red cinder driveway that cuts through them both. He watches the clouds and he watches their shadows shift and ooze across the ground. Every now and then, in the near distance, he hears a shotgun blast or a dog bark or a car race along the highway. Once, he hears someone screaming—whether at someone else or at the universe.

Days pass slowly, but not as slowly as nights, when the shadows play tricks with his mind and the stars seem to him like the vanishing atoms of the earth as it crumbles to pieces and floats away. He glances often at his watch, waiting for what, he doesn't know. Time has already run out. For the world. And for any chance of redemption on his part. He is pathetic. The fact that few are left to witness his cowardice is at least comforting. He's not a knight, not a gunslinger, not a kung fu master or spandex-clad metahuman. He's the cat on a limb they rescue. The child crying, "Help," from a flame-filled building. The princess in the tower.

He sings to himself quietly, but he can remember only fragments of lyrics, so he slips from one song to another like somebody cycling through radio stations. Christmas carols he knows. For a while, all he sings are Christmas carols.

The air grows cold. The days grow short. The ragweed and the sagebrush grow brittle. The pine trees shake off their brown needles. Mornings, the trees and the grass sparkle with frost. The sky is a dark blue tangled with cirrus clouds that resemble a torn-up spiderweb. Halloween passes without anyone knowing it, though in the seeming spirit of the season all wear their masks, the wolfman peering from a kitchen window, Frankenstein's monster digging a grave in his backyard, Dracula sitting behind the wheel of a pickup that drives up and down streets, looking for signs of life.

The power goes out. One minute refrigerators are humming, stereos playing, lamps glowing, and the next, they go dark and silent. Those who are still alive bring matches to Sternos and spark on their propane grills to cook. The growl of chainsaws fills the air as some take down the trees along the curbs, in the parks, sectioning them up into logs they can split into firewood to stay warm. So many homes have black Xs spray-painted across their doors, the hieroglyphs of the infected, most of whom are already dead. All the store windows have been broken by the bricks of looters, and in the evening the glass catches the last of the dying sunlight and winks red.

Sara has lost twenty pounds. For breakfast she has two crackers and some water. She needs to venture out again, to get food, wood, supplies for the coming winter. She still has bite and scratch marks reddening her body from the dogs, but she fought them off and it makes her feel a little braver now. She fetches her softball bat—Oathmaker—and pulls open her garage door and there they are. Maybe twenty of them. The figures are wearing masks, and they are scattered across the driveway and the lawn and the sidewalks and the street, as still as statues.

She feels her expression shift, along with her heart, as she feels confusion and then recognition and then horror. A trembling runs through her body and her voice when she says, "What do you want?"

They don't know what they have come for—except to lash out at something—but maybe seeing her now makes them realize she isn't what they are looking for after all.

"The world's starting over and you have a choice," she says, and she's proud of the steel in her voice. "You get to choose what you'll be. I'm going to choose hope. I hope you will too."

Slowly she pulls down the garage door. None of the masked figures make a move to stop her.

Up in the foothills of the Cascade Mountains there is a cave a hundred yards deep. Several families gather their rifles and sleeping bags and fill their backpacks with matches and food and clothes for all seasons and hike there to wait out the sickness. They choose the cave because it is isolated, easily defended, and maybe they choose it, too, because they feel already as though they are slipping back in history, to a simpler time dedicated to the gathering of food and the warding off of danger. They make a fire the first night and with the cinders of it draw upon the basalt walls pictures of bodies lying all about with black Xs for eyes, a cipher for future generations to behold and puzzle over.

It is colder in the cave than they imagined, and on the third day, one of their party sneaks down to the town for blankets and coats, and by the time he returns he is coughing and soon they are all dead.

A hard rain comes. It falls through broken windows and soaks carpets. It dimples the fresh earth of the graves dug all over town. At Sara's house, it tongues its way under a loose shingle and seeps through the insulation and the ceiling beneath it to form a damp circle that sags downward. Her skyscape mural—the illusion of another world—is ruined.

She paces her room, running her hands through her hair and chewing her fingernails down to nubs, feeling starved and alone, utterly alone, trapped as if in the dungeon of the evil sorcerer. It is something she has fantasized about before, something she has written about in her stories. In one of them she gnaws off her finger and uses the bone to pick the lock and then hurls the sorcerer from a window as lightning crackles from his hands. In another she writes a note in blood and tucks it under the wing of a raven who flies it to the giant bears who live in the Dire Forest and they come charging across the plains and burrow beneath the castle and into her cell and they splinter the door and overthrow the sorcerer and feast on his magical flesh and take on his powers and she becomes their queen, the queen of the bears.

But things are not so easy or so fun here in River Falls. Every time she tries to leave her house she's attacked. She might as well be guarded by wraiths or surrounded by enchanted brambles. She's always read her way out of this world. Her story will not end happily ever after unless she authors it herself.

She pulls up a chair to her desk and rips a page from a composition booklet. She grips a pen in her hand so tightly her knuckles go white. "I'm alive and I'm alone," she writes and then stops the pen. What else can she share? What else is there? Her mind is slower than it used to be, walled off from interaction, any activity outside of peering out the window, talking to herself. "I'm not sick." She underlines this twice. "Sometimes I wish I were, but I'm not. If you're alive, if you're reading this, maybe you know what I mean. I don't need you to rescue me—I'm not looking for heroes—but I sure could use some company. Because this is a lonely battle. Come find me." She lists her address. She signs her name. And she finishes the note the way she has finished every story she has ever written. "Happily ever after?" That's what she writes along the bottom, the way some would write "Regards" or "All the best" or "Love," only followed by a question mark. There are so many shadows in the world—and so little light ahead—but writing this makes her feel a little better, hopeful.

She rolls up the sheet of paper like a scroll, tapes it shut. She then stands from the desk and selects from one of the bedposts the balloon that will most likely catch someone's attention, a red balloon shaped like a heart. She bought it at Walgreens. It is a few weeks old and flaccid, but it will have to do. To its string she tapes the note several times over.

She goes down the hall to the living room and peers through the curtains for a minute—watching the wind shake the pine tree growing along the curb—before trusting the street to be empty. She opens the door and steps out onto the porch.

She holds out the balloon and scrunches shut her eyes and makes a wish—and lets go.

Once, when he was a boy, Hank found a bald eagle shot dead in the woods. He couldn't imagine anyone shooting an eagle, but there it was, a hole blasted through its middle, its feathers scorched, one of its wings still outstretched with the hope of flight. He spent a lot of time in the woods—imagining pinecones into grenades, firing slingshots at jackrabbits, hammering together forts from lumber stolen from construction sites—and he would run across the eagle often. Ants and flies stripped it of its guts and muscle. Its feathers faded and moldered and came loose, lost to the rain and wind, so that there was only the skeleton. Mud and crab-grass filled its hollows and eventually took it over entirely so that in time Hank was unable to make out any sign of it. He figured that was how he would end up, how people would end up, erased completely. The world would move on. He has never felt smaller, less substantial. He doesn't even bother with his breathing exercises anymore. There is no peach to breathe in. The whole world has gone green.

Just then he sees something. Something red. It floats along the tree line, rising with an updraft, clearing the branches that threaten to snatch it. A crosscurrent knocks it toward the meadow that surrounds his cabin, toward his porch, where it comes twisting, bullied by the wind, dropping suddenly toward him. He sets down his pistol and rips off his gas mask. He is smiling. He is holding out his arms.

One moment the balloon seems to jerk upward, and the next, he is—impossibly—grabbing it by the string. It is as if time skips. He pulls the balloon against his body, nearly crushing it in a hug. He looks at the balloon, and then at the sky, and then at the balloon, and laughs.

He looks around, startled by the sound, so alien. It takes him a moment to spot the note. It is only after he unpeels it, after he reads the message, after a smile splits his face and fresh laughter escapes his throat, that the possibility of a future begins to open back up for him, that he begins to think maybe, just maybe, he can set off for town, with his pistol ready and his eyes narrowed for danger. He can escape his tower. He can seek out this Sara. And maybe, together, they can be brave. They can find hope.

Suicide Woods

Once a month, we shrug on our backpacks and follow Mr. Engel along the trails stitching the four hundred acres of firs and hemlocks and cedars in Forest Park, which everyone calls Suicide Woods. This is on the outskirts of Portland, in the Tualatin Mountains, and within its canyons we have learned to traverse a series of switchbacks, to drop out of sunlight and into shadow. The honk and grumble of the city are replaced by the rush of Balch Creek. The wind never stops blowing here, damp and cool, shivering the branches and hushing our ears. When we talk, we whisper.

At night, some say, ghosts hang like rags in the trees. But even in the daytime we find bodies so often that Mr. Engel seems to have them marked on a map. They lie in beds of moss. They dangle from branches. We find them alone and together, clothed and naked.

The forest is so thick that weeks can pass before the dead are discovered. We leave the trails and hike ten feet apart, parting the sword ferns with walking sticks, peering into blackberry brambles. When we hear the angry buzz of flies or the crack of a gunshot, when we see vultures roosting, when we come upon a face as pale as a mushroom gaping from the undergrowth, we clump together and circle the body and hold hands and cry.

Mr. Engel says it's good to cry. He says that it's like lancing a boil, that it gets out the poisons stewing inside us. He says we need to face our emotions, and that's why he takes us here, to share with us the reality of death—the bloated faces, the soiled underwear, the skin the shade of a green-black thunderhead. He tries so hard. He wants to make us better.

There are ten or twelve or fifteen of us, our number ever fluctuating, because one of us might be in the hospital or in rehab or curled up in a corner clutching a tattered doll. Or one of us could very well be dead. Death is always a possibility. That's what unites us. That's what drew us to Mr. Engel's website—and later his home, where he hosts his weekly meetings. In all of us there is a want to drink antifreeze, to dive in front of a semi, to bring butcher knives to our wrists.

Mr. Engel wears Chuck Taylors, tight black jeans with the hems rolled up, skull T-shirts, thrift store cardigans. He dresses like he's in his twenties, but his lined face and spotted hands might indicate he's in his sixties. "Sadness ages you," he says, and he is right; though our ages vary from nineteen to seventy-two, we all suffer from the bent faces and collapsed postures of the elderly.

His wrists carry white lines on them. We are all similarly marked. There is Jean, whose neck healed crookedly after she hanged herself. There is Sam, his skull dented and bald-patched from the bullet still seeded deep in his brain. There is Denver, who makes a sound like gargling when she talks, as though she never coughed up all the pondwater she tried to drown herself in. Cara has thin, gray teeth from all the times she's puked up pills, and Mason looks like many pieces of gum chewed up and spit out from the time he took a gasoline shower and torched himself with a lit cig. It is not as easy to die as you think.

. . .

Some of us have jobs—tending bar or shelving books or roasting beans—but many of us do not. We live with our parents or we live with our siblings or we live with our adult children. They do not trust us to live alone. We fill our days with video games and YouTube clips and television programs that feature people stripping weight or hunting spouses or remodeling kitchens, fabricating a brighter life that seems unavailable to us. Sometimes we go days without talking to anyone except the pizza delivery guy.

We take Xanax. We take Lorazepam. We take Prozac and Paxil and Zoloft. Dozens of little moons dissolve inside us and make our brains deaden and our hearts fizz. Sometimes we are so sad we do not move. We will stare at the floor or the ceiling or the wall for hours, watch the shadows lean, watch a spider spin a ghostly sac around a carpenter ant. We sit so long that when we stand our muscles cramp and ache as if already succumbing to rigor mortis.

This is why Mr. Engel forces us to exercise. We take long hikes in Suicide Woods and the Columbia River Gorge and near the base of Mount Hood. He leads us blinking into the sun and charges our seizing calves and calcified spines into movement. He says that with regular exercise the heart's chambers expand, the muscle thickens. And if there is anything we need, it is more heart.

Sometimes Mr. Engel invites over instructors, a yogi or sensei, who tell us how to breathe and bend our bodies. Mr. Engel lives in a bungalow in West Linn; his living room is walled by mirrors, like a dance studio, so that when we attempt a flying crow or take a fist to the temple we can watch ourselves falling a thousand times over.

We are falling when she walks in, when she opens the door without knocking and stands framed in sunlight and says, "Am I in the right place?"

We fall in love easily. All it takes is a smile at the supermarket register, two hands reaching for the sugar at the coffeehouse, a long look in the rearview mirror, and we're yours. Though you'd never know it. We're too afraid of rejection, Mr. Engel says, so we never take risks. We never talk to the puddle-eyed girl, the dimple-cheeked guy—never ask for a number, offer to buy a drink. We watch them sidelong and for a few minutes our hearts grow full with possibility—and then they walk away and the *what-if*s and *maybe*s are replaced by *should-have*s and *might-have-been*s and we punch a mirror and watch our reflection splinter and fall apart.

Her name is Tenley. We have never met anyone named Tenley before, but we feel like we should have. The letters sound so right when set next to one another, hard in the front, buoyant in the back. There should definitely be more Tenleys in the world.

She is an art major. A photography student at Portland State. She carries a long-nosed Canon around her neck. Her skin is off-set by hair the same nightmare-black as her clothes. A nose ring and eyebrow stud catch the light and shine. She is tattooed with a Chinese character on her wrist, a strawberry ice cream cone on her biceps, a kraken with tentacles trailing up her neck. A blue teardrop drips down her cheek, and when Denver asks her about it—with her swampy, gurgling voice—when she jokes and says, "Isn't that supposed to mean you killed someone? Have you killed someone?" Tenley says, "Not yet. But I'm going to," and when we say, "Who?" she says, "Me. I'm going to kill me."

Today, when we hike Suicide Woods, Tenley joins us. She says the moss-furred branches and giant sword ferns make this place look like some kind of fairy tale; that we ought to sprinkle breadcrumbs to find our way back. We picnic on a ridge of basalt knuckling out over the drainage. While we munch our chips and snap our apples and gurgle warm water from canteens, Mr. Engel asks us to imagine our best self.

We ask him what he means and he says, "I mean you at your best. Your ideal self. Dream big. What are you doing?"

Nobody wants to go first. Nobody ever wants to go first. We lower our heads and hide behind our bangs. So he calls on us.

Sam licks the peanut butter off his teeth and says he sees himself doing two girls at once. "And they're loving it."

Mason sees himself eating a steak at a fancy restaurant, but not too fancy, not like wearing-a-jacket fancy, just fancy enough that the steak is prime and the napkins linen.

Denver says she would be in a library, one with big stained-glass windows with colored light streaming through them, reading leather-bound books in a leather-backed chair, the kind with the gold buttons.

Then Tenley speaks. "I am at Mann's Chinese Theatre in Hollywood," she says, "surrounded by movie stars in tuxedos and gowns. Someone tears open an envelope and calls my name and I climb the stairs to the stage in a strapless gold dress. The applause is thunderous. Dozens of cameras are trained on me, and tens of millions of eyes. I accept the statue. I reach into the scoop of my dress, as if to withdraw my acceptance speech, and while everyone's still expecting me to pull out a slip of paper I grab my gun. It's a Derringer. Then I bring it to my mouth and pull the trigger."

No one says anything, not until later, after we pack up our lunches and zip up our backpacks and hike farther into the woods, after we find a body in the creek with the water foaming over it. When Tenley brings her camera to her eye and begins to snap photos, Mr. Engel says, in a shout so different from his usual whispery voice that it startles us, "Why would you say that? Don't ever say that again!"

In his living room, Mr. Engel asks us to lie down and close our eyes and imagine we have been diagnosed with cancer. "You have three months to live," he says. "What will you do in that time? How will you fill what remains of your life?"

He walks among us and against the carpet his socks sizzle with electricity.

"Now you have a month. What do you do? Where do you go?"

He waits a long time between his sentences.

"Now a week. Now a day. Now ten minutes."

Our eyes are closed, but we see him through the scrim of our eyelashes when he leans over Tenley and says, "Who will you spend your time with?"

He reaches out to touch her cheek and a blue jolt erupts from his finger and makes her gasp.

We begin to watch them more carefully now, Mr. Engel and Tenley. She shows up to meetings early and leaves late. She thumbs a message on her phone and his pocket buzzes and he brings a hand to it and smiles. In his bathroom we discover another toothbrush. The bristles smell like cigarette ash.

She rides shotgun when he drives us to funerals. They sit together in the pews for the man who starved himself down to a bundle of flesh-smeared sticks, for the woman who hanged herself and now wears a turtleneck to conceal her torn windpipe, her lips superglued shut to contain her distended tongue.

One day, Tenley asks if she can take our photos. We say yes, but only if we can cover our faces, and she says okay and makes us line up. Some of us put our hands to our faces and peek through the fingers, and some of us pull our shirts up so that we appear headless. Tenley snaps and snaps and snaps.

We huddle around her and study the digital display. "You're good," we say when she clicks through the photos, some of us cast in shadow, others in light.

Then an image of Mr. Engel appears. He is sitting in bed, propped up by pillows. Shirtless. A halo of smoke blurs his face. "Oops," she says. "Went too far." She punches a button and the screen goes black.

Mr. Engel has a picture window with a bench beneath it. On the bench stands a life-size doll, a girl of about five or seven. She wears a different outfit every day: overalls, flowered skirts, white shorts with a yellow tank top. Her hair is sometimes in a braid and sometimes in pigtails and sometimes parted cleanly down the middle.

None of us have ever asked about her. But Tenley is different from the rest of us. Unafraid. She asks. She asks about the girl in the window and Mr. Engel goes quiet. His face slackens and his body withers and he stares into the middle distance and for a moment he becomes one of us, one of the group, not our leader but our peer.

"My daughter died," he says in a voice we don't recognize, a voice that sounds like something drawn from the bottom of a well. "She died three years ago and that was her doll."

Tenley touches him on the wrist, traces the scars with her fingernail, and as she does, we all feel cut to the bone.

It is then that Mr. Engel asks us to leave. He says this so quietly we are not certain he says anything at all.

Then he says it again. "Please, please, please, leave."

We haven't been there more than five minutes, we haven't even eaten the brownies or drunk the pink lemonade. We haven't dimmed the lights and passed the talking rock, an agate the size of a plum, and shared our latest nightmare. We haven't held hands and looked one another in the eye and promised to return next time. We aren't ready. We don't want to go. But we do as he tells us. We stand and file toward the door and let in a painful wedge of light. Everyone except Tenley. She remains at his side, stroking his scars, until he rips away from her and sweeps his hand like a scythe and says, "You too."

A week passes before we hear from Mr. Engel, and when we do, his email is full of exclamation marks. He writes that he has been planning something for us! Something special! And he can't wait to show us! An overnight getaway!

In the past he used exclamation marks sparingly. We are worried. We go to him, not wanting help, but wanting to help him.

It rains here as many days as it doesn't. The sky is as gray as the pavement. Moss furs roofs. Mold breathes out of basements.

We step out of Mr. Engel's van into a spitting mist. We approach the wrought-iron gate that runs along the parking lot. Lone Fir Cemetery, the sign reads.

Mr. Engel's smile trembles at the corners when he says he has a surprise for us. He says to follow him. We do. We always do. One sleeve of his cardigan is shorter than the other and he keeps pulling at a loose string, unwinding the fabric further, revealing his scars.

A backhoe has carved out thirteen holes. Beside each of them rises a mound of dirt squirming with worms. The headstones are blank. Inside a white tent—the kind you'd see at a catered wedding—sit thirteen coffins with their lids gaping.

"Who died?" we ask.

"You did!" he says and we see then that the coffins are empty.

He says he will outfit us with an oxygen tank, Clif Bars, a water bottle. We will spend the night six feet under. We will be buried alive. His voice wavers with excitement when he says this will be a kind of final test, and though it will be uncomfortable, we will return from the experience with a better appreciation for life. He wants so badly for this to be a good idea, and we want to believe in him. He burrows his hands into the pockets of his sulfur-yellow cardigan. "So who's first?"

Of course Tenley volunteers. Who else among us would be so willing? She does not smile, but gives us the thumbs-up before we close the lid on her. We shoulder the weight of the coffin and carry it to the grave. With ropes we lower it into the muddy cavity, and with shovels we drop dirt over her until she vanishes. Mr. Engel slips the backhoe driver two twenties and he takes care of the rest.

It is hard to tell, over the noise of the engine, but we think we hear screaming.

Then it is our turn.

One night feels like many. We try to sleep, but in our dreams the walls narrow, the ceilings lower. Every breath is dirt-scented. Our eyes forget color; we do not know whether they are open or closed. There is no clock ticking off the minutes, no streetlamp glowing in the window, no sound except our panicked breathing as we imagine the worms tunneling toward us.

Maybe for the first time, we feel afraid to die.

Oxygen hisses through our masks. Whatever you do, Mr. Engel warned us, do not touch the tank. Even if you feel like you're choking, you aren't. Fiddle with the settings, though, and you will run out of air. But with the masks pressed to our mouths and our lungs gulping, we can't help but feel certain he is wrong. He is wrong and we are going to die and this is what awaits us, this is what death is.

We want the backhoe driver to wake up, finish his coffee and cigarette, key the engine. We want Mr. Engel to pull his hands out of his pockets and get to work shoveling. And then, one by one, we hear a scrape, a thud, voices. The sun blinds us and we blink our eyes at shutter-speed. Our muscles cry out with the wonderful pain of movement. We weep and clumsily applaud and strangle one another into hugs. "I'm so happy," we say. "I'm so fucking happy!"

The ground is marshy but the rain has stopped. The sun burns through a hole in the clouds. One more grave remains; the backhoe grumbles and carves up four feet of dirt as black and sticky as a chocolate cake. We drop into the pit and shovel off the rest, our blades sending up sparks when they clash. The coffin takes shape beneath us; we kneel and wipe away the dirt and knock at the lid and say, "Tenley! You did it, Tenley!"

It takes another five minutes to arrange the ropes, to haul the coffin from the hole, and by then we all feel giddy, exhilarated. When we undo the clasp, the coffin opens with a sucking sound.

"Oh no," Mr. Engel says. "No, no, no."

The satin is shredded. Her fingernails are broken and rimmed with blood. Her skin is as sepia-toned as an old photo, except for her tattoos, the teardrop on her cheek as blue as a speck of sky. On one side of her sits the oxygen tank—knobbed to its highest setting, emptied too early—and on the other, her camera, its final photo one of darkness.

Mr. Engel keeps saying, "No." But he should be saying, Yes. Because we look at her and know he was right. His efforts have paid off. We are better. He has made us better. We have never felt more repulsed by death. We have never felt so terribly alive.

The Uncharted

In her childhood bedroom, Michelle papered one wall entirely with maps. She collected them from her grandmother's *National Geographic* magazines. She tore them from her library's world atlas and the gas station's rack of Rand McNallys. She bought them for a quarter from garage sales and thrift shops. She loved the old tattered yellow explorers' maps, because they made her dream of long ago and far away, and she loved the crisp, tidily folded road maps for their detail and clarity. But she especially loved a staggered collage she tacked up—of the globe, and then the United States, and then the state of Illinois, and then the city of Chicago. She made an X on each of them that indicated where she lived. She knew exactly where she belonged when she stood before it.

Now Michelle works in Silicon Valley and lives in San Francisco, a city that makes no sense. The streets—and the landscape—wander and bend in every direction, so that she sometimes feels as if she's fallen into the upside-down topography of one of those M. C. Escher prints that some child has crayoned all over.

There's nothing wrong with being particular. That's what Michelle often tells herself. She wakes up at six and goes to bed at eleven every day. She irons her clothes and delights in the crispness of her jeans when she pulls them on. She buys segmented plates because she prefers her food not mix. She had all the hardware and fixtures in her apartment changed out to brushed steel so that they matched.

She calls it a dream job, her position at Atlas, a mapmaking tech firm popular for its navigation app and satellite-view maps. Their vans roam city streets and country highways across the world, all with camera units stationed on top that record a 360-degree view.

She is the field director of the Titan program. Her division uses the same camera technology as the vans—except on backpacks. Their goal is to map every inch of the planet. Every reef, every alleyway, every canyon. Everything. She has teams stationed in Marrakech, Bogotá, Reykjavík, the Great Barrier Reef, and beyond.

And one of them has gone missing. A team of four assigned to a northwestern sector of Alaska. Every evening they were supposed to uplink their data to the satellite, but sometimes teams in remote areas ran into problems—inclement weather, damaged equipment—so she tried not to worry at first. But after forty-eight hours passed, her panic heightened and made her lungs feel like tiny paper sacks with holes in them. Not only had her team failed to uplink, but their geo-locaters gave off no signal. They had gone dark.

Even if she'd had access to the final minutes of footage, the jumble of images probably would have confused her, like a torn-up map that didn't align with any compass.

The four team members were spread out in a line, twenty yards apart, hiking through a maze of hemlocks and cedars crowned by mossy branches and skirted by sword ferns. There were three men and one woman, all in their twenties, dirt-smeared and tromping along in boots and canvas pants and thermal long-sleeves. They paced one another, marching through the woods like patrolling soldiers.

Their backs were bent from the weight of their Titan packs, each one with a camera unit that spun on a pole like a disco globe. It was studded with lenses that reflected the dazzle of sunlight. When in motion, it made a rusty chirping sound, like many crickets sawing their legs at once.

The wind whispered and the branches swayed and the shadows shifted and a two-toned whistle sounded. Maybe a bird. Or maybe not. The team did not appear to notice. They swatted at mosquitoes. They swigged from canteens. They studied the thick undergrowth before them, trying not to stumble.

Then one of them passed behind a tree, and never showed up on the other side of it. Gone.

A few paces later, the same thing happened to another. He was there. And then he was not.

The two remaining hikers continued forward unknowingly, until a few paces later, one of them jerked out of sight. Dragged down. He gave a strangled cry, and the remaining hiker paused. And looked around. But there was nothing to see. "Paul?" he said. "Sammy?"

The camera on his back whirred in dizzying circles. As if to follow it, he turned quickly. Branches spiked toward him. Shadows pooled beneath trees and bushes. His heel caught on a root and he nearly fell. "Jane? Where are you?" His eyes blinked rapid-fire. His breathing sharpened. "Guys?"

He reached back and shut off the camera unit. The chirping ceased. The spinning globe went dead. "Hey!"

At first there was no response except the shushing wind, and then the two-toned whistle sounded again. He jerked toward it, his focus settling on a tree. One larger than the rest. With a night-black hollow in its base.

And—maybe?—something shifted inside. "Guys?" he said and unbelted his knife and cocked his head. "Where did you go?" He continued toward the tree, toward the hollow, until he crept inside, throated by darkness.

It's easy to find someone who wants to work in Istanbul or Seoul or Mexico City, humping the Titan pack into mosques and along rivers and through plaza markets. But it's nearly impossible to find someone willing and able to spend several months mountaineering in Chile or mucking through the Louisiana bayou. Michelle reached out to veterans who served in elite units, to the Sierra Club and Outward Bound programs for outdoorsy preservationists, to REI for employee sponsorship and ad revenue, and even to GoPro daredevils on YouTube.

That's how she found Josh Wilde, a twenty-two-year-old social media influencer with more than two million followers. Unlike so many of the morons online, he didn't post prank videos or goofball skits. His channel was called Gone Wilde, and over the past four years, he had hang glided over active volcanoes and dived shipwrecks and free-climbed El Capitan.

They met at the X Games, where GoPro was touting his latest stunt: wing-suiting off the Empire State Building and hurtling through the windowed canyons of Manhattan before landing at a sprint in Central Park.

He looked older than he was, tanned and sinewy, his skin creased from all his time outside, exposed to extreme temperatures. No tattoos, only scars. He kept his head buzzed down to a brown bristle.

At the GoPro pavilion she asked him out for a drink, and he said, "Just to be clear, I'm not going to work for you," and she surprised herself by saying, "Then I guess we'll have to talk about something else."

He looked at her differently then, as if she was finally coming into focus, and she thought he was going to laugh and say he had other plans, but instead he offered her a real smile along with the time and place they should meet.

It was one of those nights that she never allowed herself. She didn't like loud bars and she rarely drank anything but white wine, but they ended up at a crowded tiki lounge sipping ridiculous cocktails out of coconuts.

Josh looked like a raft guide who would pull you out of a hairy stretch of white water. He belonged in an REI catalog, standing on a summit he'd conquered and staring off at the horizon as if imagining what challenge he might take on next. "You're the Captain Kirk of outdoorsmen," she said and he said, "What?" and she said, "Nothing."

She cleaned her glasses so many times that the cocktail napkin she was using disintegrated. She had been on five dates over the past five years—was that even what this was? a date?—and never really thought about sex except when watching shows on premium cable.

It wasn't long before she felt the warmth of the rum buzzing her nerves and spreading to the tips of her fingers. Josh wasn't like so many of the other men she hired. He didn't try to show off or brag. He barely seemed aware of himself. His T-shirt had a hole in it. One of his nails was black and looked ready to fall off. He was missing a molar. He smelled like he had swiped on some deodorant but forgotten to shower. She was looking for reasons not to like him, but none of them convinced her. She talked for over an hour, in a chirpy, harried voice, about mapmaking technology before asking him, "How did you end up doing what you're doing? Are you crazy or something?"

He laughed and shook his head and his palm made a scraping sound when he ran it across his scalp.

"Sorry," she said. "That was a terrible question. This rum, it's—"

"It's all good."

"No, forget it. I—"

"It wasn't my idea. It was my friends'." He motioned to the bartender then, requesting another round. His voice softened when he said, "They thought it was the best way to keep me from killing myself."

In high school, he'd survived a car crash. His parents and sister hadn't. They were driving the Santiam Pass in Oregon. Six inches of snow had fallen and the plows hadn't caught up. Their Jeep slid off the road on a curve and crashed down a five-hundred-foot embankment and finally came to a rest half-sunken in a river. His father drowned. His mother was thrown from the passenger window. His sister's arm was cloven off and she bled to death. And Josh was knocked unconscious, dangling upside down by his seat belt, with more than twenty broken bones. The snow covered up the skid marks. Two days passed before an elk hunter discovered him.

Some people said it was a miracle he had survived. Others said he was unkillable. "It's almost like I wanted to prove them wrong."

He started free-climbing buildings, kayaking off waterfalls, cave diving, and then his friends Todd Dartman and Lester Grimson sat him down and asked him what the hell he was doing. "The only time I felt alive was when I was nearly dead," he told them.

It didn't make any sense. Not to Michelle. Not even in the slightest. Roller coasters made her weep. And driving the freeway, with cars ripping in and out of the lanes, put her in a vomity panic. She hated speed, risk, chaos. But as he continued to speak, she felt herself nodding her head. And she watched—somewhat terrified—as her hand rose to his shoulder. She began to stroke, then knead the muscle there.

Josh's friends knew they couldn't keep him from doing what he was doing, so they were going to accompany him. Plan and manage his itinerary. Spot him. Bail him out if he got into trouble. The monetization of the whole thing came by accident, after Todd posted a video that went viral of Josh mountain biking off a ski jump.

"Anyway," he said, "I don't know why I'm telling you any of this. Sorry."

"No," she said. "Don't apologize. Thank you so much."

"Why are you thanking me?"

"Because—I don't know—I'm just from the stupid suburbs."

"What?"

"I'm like everybody else. You're not. That's why people like watching you. Because it's good to be reminded that there are other ways to live. That you don't have to sit at a desk all day and worry about your retirement savings or whatever."

She always kept her hair in a severe ponytail and she noticed then a few stray hairs clinging to the sweat on her cheek and slipped the band off to tighten it again and he said, "Don't," and she said,

"Don't what?" and he said, "You look good with your hair down," and then he reached out and combed his fingers through it and his scarred-up knuckles brushed her cheek and she whispered, "Why not?" and it wasn't long before they were hurrying to pay the check.

It's been over a year since that night. Maybe he doesn't even remember her. She doesn't have his email or phone number, and she snuck out of his hotel room before he woke up. Not because she was embarrassed or regretful. But because she wanted to preserve that happy, heated feeling and not let it be ruined by the awkwardness of saying, "So long" and acknowledging nothing could ever work out between them. Her heart was a territory that would remain unexplored.

But now her team has gone missing and not even Alaska's 212th Rescue Squadron has been able to locate them. She needs Josh Wilde.

The sky's reflection glimmers on the water. White collars of foam curl around boulders. Roots tangle the banks. The river's murmur gives way to a roar where it spills over into a curiously forked waterfall.

To one side, the river drops thirty feet into a shushing boom of mist and roiling water. And to the other side, the river plummets into a gaping chasm, the entrance to an underground tunnel. This is the Devil's Kettle, in northern Minnesota.

Todd Dartman balances on the rocks here. He is the kind of guy who incorrectly quotes passages from *On the Road*. Bleach-haired, soul-patched, potbellied. He wears a hemp necklace and a Phish T-shirt, and has hazy memories of every youth hostel in Europe.

He's geared out with electronics. A Bluetooth headset. And a shoulder-mounted GoPro camera that's currently live-streaming. A climbing rope and harness anchor him to the shore. He is the voice of Gone Wilde, and he says, "All right, friends and brethren. We're about five minutes out from our latest stunt. Hope you're hungry for a triple cheeseburger of terror, adrenaline, and life-threatening awesomeness." He stutters his feet to the edge and peers down into the kettle. "You see that? Looks like certain death to me. A river to nowhere."

Then another voice crackles over the Bluetooth. Lester. "You ready to do something stupid?" he says.

"Always!" Todd says. "We're good to go on this end. You in position?"

Lester is. About a mile from shore, on the blue calm of Lake Superior, a boat drops anchor, the metal weight cutting through the water. He waits for the line to go slack as the anchor clanks the rocky bottom. He wears cargo shorts and a collared shirt with many pockets. He styles his hair in a black puff, a kind of helmet that he can stick a pen or pencil into. He, too, is live-streaming from a camera unit vised to the dashboard of the bowrider.

The deck is cluttered with recording equipment, a first aid kit, a heart defibrillator, a cooler, snorkel gear. Right now Lester is consulting his GPS feed, a green-screened tablet that lists his coordinates. "I'm anchored over the tunnel system's spout. All goes well, he should spring up nearby. *If* all goes well."

Todd says, "Four miles of underground tunnels blasting ice-cold water along at forty miles an hour. What could go wrong?"

Lester's face pinches with worry. "Everything."

He hears a noise then. The whump-whump-whump of an approaching helicopter. He makes his hand into a visor. "Chopper's rolling in. Might be we're about to get busted."

"More drama means more coverage," Todd says. "More coverage means more subscribers means more ad dollars."

"Yeah, well," Lester says. "Let's just hope we're not making a snuff video. Our boy Josh has used up his nine lives at this point."

Upriver from the Devil's Kettle, Josh roams the banks, collecting rocks to puzzle together into a cairn. It's already waist-high. Lichen-crusted and mud-slimed. Gapped with shadows. This is his ritual before every stunt. He is about to dive into the void and dare the underwater tunnel system that veins its way into Lake Superior.

His helmet camera is powered off and waiting on the bank. This moment belongs to him alone. He is bare-chested, the dry suit peeled to his waist. He adds another rock, then another. It's a little like digging his own grave. Makes him realize what's at risk. Reminds him there's still time to back out, and more and more, he's eager to back out. At first what he was doing felt like some sort of atonement. Now it just feels stupid. But he and his friends have built this . . . *thing* together. Whatever it is. A business? A micro media empire? Somehow a bunch of dumbass high school graduates are pulling in mid–six figures a year off ad revenue from GoPro, Clif Bar, and Patagonia, among other brands. Initially this was supposed to be for Josh, but it increasingly feels like it's for them.

His friends call him a warrior poet. They have misinterpreted his emptiness for depth. Vacant is how he feels most of the time. Hollow. Carved out. Sure, he'll throw up his pinky and index fingers in the shape of the devil's horns and say something for the camera, like: "Let's own this mountain," or "Ride the razor's edge," or whatever bullshit. But it's all an act. He doesn't give two damns.

His body is crosshatched with scars, but there's one that stands out from the rest. A thick, gummy line that runs from his collarbone to his hip. It came from the car wreck and the surgery that followed. A daily reminder that he lived and his family didn't. If he dug into it with a knife, nothing would dribble out of him but stale air and shadows. He would simply deflate.

So many people told Josh he must have lived for a reason. He must have some purpose to fulfill before death could finally claim him. They were wrong. He performs stunts that people watch on their phones while waiting for the bus or taking a shit. His life is meaningless, and yet everyone treats him like he's something special.

Todd hollers his way, indicating it's go time, and Josh lifts a hand to acknowledge him before adding one last agate—a milky yellow nugget—to the top of the cairn. Then he sockets his arms into the sleeves of his dry suit and slowly zips the chest shut. For the kettle run, Lester built him custom-made aquatic shoes that give him the appearance of having long, webbed toes. And a custom oxygen tank—heavily padded and smaller than a standard scuba— that Josh shoulders now before splashing his way downstream.

Todd trains the camera on Josh and throws up a celebratory fist and speaks in a fight announcer's voice. "Here comes the man of the hour! He wing-suited off the Empire State Building, he free-climbed El Capitan, he hang glided over the lava-spewing belly of Mount Kilauea. Josh motherfucking Wilde!"

This is Josh's cue. He's supposed to say something badass, something they can print on coffee mugs and T-shirts and sell off the website. But all he can manage is a smile.

So Todd talks for him. "Never feel so jacked up as when you tease death, am I right? Wag your tongue in the reaper's face? Josh?"

In response Josh pulls on his mask. Then fits on the helmet with the camera and high-powered LED lamp attached to it.

"Josh?" Todd slaps him on the shoulder. "You ready to dare the nightmare, bro?"

Josh hops up and down, shakes out his arms, cracks his neck. Then he looks long and hard at Todd. "I think this is it," he says.

"Dude, you'll be fine. You're always fine."

"No," Josh says. "I mean . . . I think I'm done? I think I'm ready to not do this anymore."

Todd's voice reveals that he might be not only confused, but also hurt. "But . . . what? Why?"

Josh tucks in his mouthpiece. Heaves a fat dose of oxygen. And jumps into nothingness. The whitewater seizes him and drags him down into the underworld.

For a few seconds he sees nothing, lost in the black nowhere of an underground channel. He hears the burbling rush and hiss of water. He feels the current shoving him along. And then, in flashes, the tunnel comes into focus and he finds his bearings. This is the world's deadliest waterslide, and he's blasting through it like a bullet down a gun barrel.

Millions of tons of rock surround him. He could be a mile or more beneath the ground. This is an unrecoverable, unimaginable place. No one can save him if something goes wrong—and that recognition makes him feel suddenly alive. It's a rarer and rarer sensation. He's mostly lost his capacity for awe. But now, as if a button has been pushed, every nerve in his body lights up like a circuit board. He lets out a whoop of delight, muffled by his regulator.

Against a sharp turn in the tunnel he clangs and loses his breath. He barely recovers before wheeling around and striking the opposite wall so hard that little galaxies of light spin through his vision. In a wrenching second, he comes to a painful stop.

At first it appears—in the glow of his lamplight—to be a tangle of branches that blocks his passage. But as he readjusts himself, he sees it's a deer. A dead buck with a wide rack of antlers. Its rotten face stares back at him with bone whitening through the flesh. Like something demonic, elemental.

Josh startles, and recovers from his fright, but he can't get loose, the straps for the oxygen tank caught up in the horns. The water drags hard at him. As if he were a salmon struggling at the end of a hooked line. The deer's carcass flops against his, the antlers prodding him.

He tries to unclip his tank. And can't. For a moment, he considers giving up. Wouldn't that be a relief? To end? Fifteen minutes ago that might have been the case, but right now he's never been so happily, painfully alive. So he reaches for a belt knife. Snicks the blade through a strap. As it severs, his body flops painfully sideways, still caught in the current.

He slashes the other strap—and away he swirls. His mouthpiece rips away with the tank and he's thrown down the tunnel with one last gulp of air to sustain him.

The boat rocks when Lester hurries from starboard to port and back again, saying, "Shit, shit, shit." He peers into the bright blue water, hunting for bubbles, some blurred movement, anything. "Should have come up by now."

Over the headset, Todd says, "You do this every time, Lester. Just chill. Stop being such a mom. Our boy'll be fine."

Thirty yards away, the helicopter lowers its pontoons to the water. The engine powers down.

"What about now?" Todd says. "Now is when I would maybe start to feel worried."

"Still nothing. He's a minute past now. He could be caught up in the tunnel or knocked out right beneath the boat for all I know. Can't see for shit because of the rotor wash coming off the chopper. I'm going in."

With that Lester rips off his earpiece, kicks off his shoes, and pulls on a snorkel and mask. Just as he swings his leg over the rail, some bubbles bother the surface of the lake.

Right then, with a sucking gasp of air, Josh breaches the surface. Closer to the chopper than the boat. He leans back and breathes greedily and gives Lester a tired wave. "I'm," Josh says, "here."

"You're crazy," Lester says. "You're a crazy bastard!"

Josh is the face of their operation. And the balls. Todd is their mascot, narrator, and cheerleader. And Lester? He's the guy at the desk. He produces and edits the videos, manages their finances, plots their trips, and engineers any specialized gear for the stunts. He doesn't take risks. He doesn't even particularly like to exercise. But there's something about working with Josh that jacks up his pulse and makes him feel a vicarious thrill. It's the equivalent of playing video games or watching movies—which he allots a lot of time to—except that he's truly complicit in the adventure, and if he doesn't take the necessary precautions, the hero could actually die.

Once again, the hero survived, and Lester is so relieved, he leaps fully clothed into the water, laughing and yelping at the coldness of it. "You made it," Lester says, paddling over to him. "You scared the hell out of me, pal."

Josh floats on his back, coughing and sputtering water through his smile. "I scared the hell out of me too."

The helicopter has powered down completely. The water laps against its floats. The passenger door rolls open with a clank. Someone—a young woman with Chuck Taylors and skinny jeans and chunky black glasses and a ponytail—stands on the other side of it. Lester assumes she's a reporter, until he sees the windbreaker shell that reads Titan across the chest, alongside the program's compass emblem. She tips her head and says, "Remember me?"

Josh straightens his body and scissors his legs and spits out a mouthful of water and squints against the sun's glare. "Michelle?"

"Surprise," she says.

"But," Josh says, "what are you doing here?"

She reaches out a hand and beckons him with a curl of her fingers. "I came to offer you a job."

A day later, in Mountain View, California, she escorts them into the Atlas boardroom, and they take their seats at the long black table that runs the length of it. Josh, Lester, and Todd. Unshaven, in their outdoor gear and with slumped postures, they look at odds with the sterile environment.

One wall is a whiteboard. The other three are made up of floor-to-ceiling windows that look out on the sunlit campus, which has the appearance of a futuristic college studded with palm trees. A manicured paradise. Every afternoon, Michelle takes a fast walk, following the looping concrete pathways through the rock and flower gardens, until her Fitbit tells her she's burned a lunch's worth of calories. She checks it now and sees that her heart rate has elevated to 120, though she's standing still.

Maybe it's the guilt over losing her team. Or maybe it's the fear that these three will turn her down. Or maybe it's just Josh. Her eyes keep coming back to him, though there are so many other places to look.

She crosses her arms, then remembers the TED Talk she watched, and hurries her hands to her hips instead and broadens her stance to a power pose. Now she's in control. Josh arches his crowbar of an eyebrow at her and somehow she doesn't feel reassured.

A laptop sits on the table beside her and she punches the keyboard with her finger to warm it up. "The Last Frontier," she says.

Todd throws up his arms. "Space?! We're going to space!"

"Alaska."

His arms flop down. "Oh."

Her laptop is connected to a ceiling projector that beams an image onto the wall. The Atlas emblem on a black banner. Below it is a man standing on the summit of a mountain, with the camera unit lodged in his pack.

This gives way to a series of moving images. Starting with the Grand Canyon. The classic sweeping view from above, and then the vantage drops down onto a trail and explores the interior, sliding past scrub brush and sandy washes and the layers and layers of rock that mark the descent.

She explains how, with Titan's help, you can be a virtual tourist, a student of the world, from the comfort of your home or classroom. And the images shift over to a plaza in Italy and the camera creeps inside of a restaurant, through the seating area, into the kitchen, and then the alleyway behind it. And then the images shift again to churches and bars and museums of Sicily. And again to a white sand beach in Costa Rica that runs up against a pale blue ocean.

Michelle directs the navigation down the beach and then into the water. They slide through a candy-colored reef. Striped fish gather in schools. An eel peers out of a tiny cave. Anemones wave in the current. A sea turtle tips toward the camera curiously.

"Forget Alaska," Todd says. "We should go there. Hang out with some hula girls and drink some unnaturally blue cocktail out of a giant-ass glass with lots of umbrellas."

Lester elbows him and says, "Listen to the lady."

She says, "Anybody can wander a beach with a camera. We tapped you guys for a reason."

Lester is only half-joking when he says, "Because we're—what?—the suicide squad?" He has a tic, she notices, on his left cheek.

"We've so far mapped every inch of North America. Except . . ." She swipes at the mouse pad and calls up a map of Alaska and zooms in on a highlighted area that looks like a fanged mouth. "Except for this section of the Alaskan coastline. Which is—full disclosure—known as the Bermuda Triangle of the North. Hundreds go missing there every year."

"Um," Todd says, and she hurries on before he can undercut her with a joke.

"Single-engine flights, commercial fishing boats. Hunters, hikers, campers, mining and logging prospectors."

Outside, a cloud scuds across the sun and the boardroom falls into a gloom.

Josh finally speaks. When he does, Todd and Lester swing their faces toward him. His voice is low, almost gravitational. She hates that he owns them the same as he owns her. "So you think we're the only ones crazy enough to go there?"

"Or stupid enough," Lester says.

Michelle eyes Josh for a long beat. She doesn't want to tell them. She doesn't want to send them. But she has to. It's her job. "I don't think you're the only ones." Her eyes drop and her body goes wooden. "We . . . lost a team there last month."

Lester's tic goes wild, his left cheek tightening and releasing, over and over, as if he's trying and failing to form a smile. Todd leans back and snorts out a laugh. But Josh maintains his steady gaze.

"Lost? As in, they might still be alive?"

"At this point . . ." Her throat feels too dry for words. "I think that's extremely doubtful. But I have to hope."

Lester puts a hand over his cheek to massage the muscle, control the tic. "Oh, this sounds wonderful. Sign me up."

Josh says, "You couldn't track their sat phones or GPS units?"

"They went dark. And all recovery efforts by local rescue teams have failed." There's a long moment of quiet. "Look. Someone's going to do this. It's happening. And it's not that I think you're stupid enough to go there. It's that I think you're smart enough to get out."

"So we're searching while we're recording?" Josh says.

"Correct. It's a walk-and-chew-gum deal. To cover the area completely should take you four weeks."

Lester says, "What Todd said before? About the coconuts? I agree. Let's go there instead."

Josh puts a calming hand on Lester's shoulder. "What do you think happened? To them? To anybody else who has gone missing or died there?"

Michelle shakes her head, unsure. "Brutal weather. Bears. Wolves. No roads. No nautical charts. No cell signal. No nothing for hundreds of miles."

Todd says, "Bermuda Triangle of the North, man. Supernatural vortex. That's what did it."

Michelle says, "You know what they used to write on old maps, at the end of the known world—"

Josh finishes the sentence for her. "Here there be dragons."

"Yeah." She tries to smile, but the darkness of what's promised makes her mouth tremble. "This is where you find the dragons."

Josh doesn't look at the contracts Michelle hands out. Not even when Todd whistles long and low and says, "That's like fifty hot tubs. Full of Dom Pérignon." The money doesn't matter to him. It's the danger he finds appealing, yes, but more so the mission. To save someone.

For whatever reason, ever since the car wreck, he's been fixated on how *he* should have died—instead of recognizing that his family should have lived. He can't go back in time and slam the brakes or wrench the steering wheel in another direction. But he can do this.

"No," Lester says. "Absolutely not. We're not doing it."

"Why?"

"Because that's not what we do."

"Maybe that's a good thing," Josh says.

"I don't understand." A cluster of water bottles sits at the center of the table, like a blue bouquet, and Lester rips the cap off one of them and guzzles. "We've got a business model that works. We—"

"We make stupid videos and earn money off endorsement deals from energy drinks," Josh says, and he can see the hurt in Lester's expression, but it doesn't stop him. "I'm sick of it. Let's do something substantial for a change."

"But, Josh," Todd says, his voice uncharacteristically quiet, almost solemn. "Me and Lester . . . we're not really equipped for this kind of thing."

Josh realizes then how parasitic they are. It's not that they aren't his friends. It's not that they haven't carried him through rough times. But they've made a lot of money off him repeatedly failing to kill himself.

A part of him wants to sign the contract for obvious reasons. Dare the wilderness and locate the lost team. And another part of him—a hidden, nasty part of him—likes the idea of putting his friends in harm's way.

"Then I'll go alone," Josh says, knowing they'll follow him anywhere.

"Whoa," Lester says. "No. Let's just hold on a minute." He neatens the contract before him and blows out a steadying breath and looks at Michelle and says, "We'll do it, but only if we retain rights to the footage."

"This isn't entertainment," she says.

"You're wrong about that," he says. "People love horror movies."

She agrees, but before they sign anything, she wants to give them one final chance to say no. "It's okay," she says. "You don't have to do this."

That's how they end up at the Lake Hood Seaplane Base, in Anchorage, Alaska, two days later. On the water, the floatplanes taxi, with hundreds of them docked along the shore. Some of the aircraft are high-end, but more of them look like they're barely held together by duct tape. Rust-streaked with mismatched replacement panels.

Inside a nearby hangar, they stand around a pile of duffels and backpacks and bear bags and scuba gear.

Josh hefts up the Titan pack and swings it onto his back. The giant ball of the many-lensed camera rises from a metal proboscis, reaching two feet higher than his head. He readjusts the beltline, and leans one way, then the other, and pops out an experimental squat. "How does it feel?" Lester says and Josh says, "Like I got a gargoyle on my back."

"Quit whining," Michelle says. "Come here." She tightens the shoulder straps and snaps the chest harness into place. Her hands linger there for a moment, as if she can feel his heart in her fingers. "How's that? Will you live?"

"Remains to be seen," Josh says.

At this she flinches and drops her hands. "Don't say that, please," she says to him, and then to the group, "You'll each have your own pack. I recommend hiking twenty yards apart in wooded areas, and swimming ten yards apart in water, making patterned sweeps for total coverage. In addition to the camera, you've got a GPS antenna in there to geo-locate all the photos. A fat battery that should last a week before you trade it out. And an SSD on the bottom for storage."

Lester checks everything over and nods approvingly. "Clunky but cool." He snaps on a button and the camera powers up and begins to spin and emits a noise like a cricket's chirping.

"So the camera unit fires every two seconds," Michelle says, "giving a panoramic view of wherever you hike, swim, canoe, bike, snowmobile, ski." She holds out a thickly armored satellite phone. "This satellite phone is your lifeline. Anything goes wrong, you let me know."

Lester snatches this from her, examines it, tucks it in one of his many pockets. "Given where we're headed, isn't that pretty much a guarantee?"

Todd says, "We'll be fine, old lady Lester. I eat a bowl of grizzly bears doused in gasoline for breakfast every morning."

Michelle claps her hands and waves for them to follow her

across the hangar. "All right, boys. Follow me and I'll introduce you to your bush pilot."

Josh watches her go. She has such a stiff, precise manner. Even when she walks, she brings down her heel sharply with each step, as if she were stomping ants. He remembers how all of that melted away in the hotel room. She insisted on turning off the lights, and it was almost as if she needed that camouflage to become something else. A wild thing. She was gone when he woke up, but the claw marks weren't.

Lester turns off the camera and helps him unshoulder the pack and lower it to the floor. "Four weeks of mosquitoes, no showers, no pizza. The threat of a supernatural vortex that eats ships, planes, and people."

"Sounds like fun?"

"No. It does not."

"And yet, here you are," Josh says.

"I wasn't going to let you go alone. And, I'll admit, it's somewhat exciting to think about us belonging to the last generation of explorers."

"Looking to join the ranks of Magellan, Sir Walter Raleigh, and Lewis and Clark?"

"Or, " Lester says, "maybe we can avoid the whole colonizer thing. Think I'd prefer the company of Armstrong and Cousteau."

"Good call." Josh nods at Todd, who at that moment is bending over to zip up a bag. His pants sag with the effort, revealing a pale slab of skin and the crack of his ass. "Armstrong. Cousteau. Now we can add to that list the esteemed Todd Dartman."

The bush pilot's name is Cliff Swanson, and he thinks they're all a bunch of idiots. He tells them as much, even though they're paying him well. Twice his standard rate. "Hypothermia. Moose attack. Bear attack. Wolf attack. Avalanche. Starvation. Giardia. Drowning." They follow him as he marches toward the plane, and every few steps he turns to admonish them directly. "Eat the wrong berry, you're dead. Fall off a cliff, you're dead. Misfire your rifle, you're dead. There are a million ways this place will kill you."

They all wear shoulder-mounted GoPro cameras, and Todd runs ahead of Cliff and then turns around and walks backward, so as to film him. "We'll be all right, big guy. We've been to some pretty hairy places."

Cliff holds up his hand as if to block the camera. "This isn't some dumb movie. And we're not headed to some Maui poolside bar or a Bangkok whorehouse or wherever else you've been on your party boy vacations. This isn't even Alaska. It's the *jaws* of Alaska."

"Chill," Todd says. "We got this."

Michelle says, "I don't think you do. Not with that attitude."

"Listen to the lady," Cliff says.

"I know this must seem scary," Josh says to Michelle, "to someone like you. But—"

"To someone like me?"

"Yeah, someone who lives—"

She was walking beside him, but now the distance between them grows and she looks at him with sidelong annoyance. "And how would you define someone like me?"

"Someone who lives . . . a safety-padded, seat-belted, air-conditioned life."

Michelle's face pinches and Todd hurries over to her and says, "He's mean. That's why you should like me. I'm nice. And cuddly."

"Don't act like you know me," Michelle says. "And don't act like you're too cool to die out there." She flicks the GoPro camera on his shoulder. "It's like Cliff says. This isn't some dumb movie."

Cliff starts off again, machine-gunning them with his words. "They call this state the Last Frontier for a reason, you know. It's unconquered." None of them get it, he says. Nobody from the Lower 48 does. They're used to conquering. Dirt is something to pave over. Wood is something to split and sand and lacquer into furniture. A mountain is something to ski down. The land here does the same thing to people—owns and consumes them. He was part of the search party for the last group. He doesn't want to do that again, crisscrossing the skies and hoping for an SOS. Maybe if he puts the fear of God into them, they'll be more cautious.

He tromps along the dock and approaches his single-engine floatplane. He knows it looks like it's been through a few dogfights. Patched and soldered. But it does the job. Has done it for the twenty years he's been flying. He yanks open the cargo door with a shriek. Motions for them to give him their bags. The Titan pack weighs a good fifty pounds, and for a moment he considers tossing it in the water.

But then Michelle says, "Please be careful with that," and he seems to remember that she's the one who writes the checks and so he gently places the equipment in the hold, along with the rest of the gear, before bungee cording it all tightly into place.

Usually Michelle is all business. Buttoned-up, tightly wound. But today she feels rickety and nerve-baked. She doesn't want to say good-bye. It feels likes too dangerous of a word. So she says, "Okay, boys," walking backward and giving them a half wave. "Please stay safe? When you touch down, ping me on the satellite phone."

But before she can retreat any farther, Josh grabs her hand, hooking their fingers together. "Hey," he says, and she says, "Hey?"

She tries not to pay attention to Todd and Lester as they smile and whisper at each other. She tries to look into his eyes and hold her gaze steady. "Hey?" he says.

"Hey."

"I'm sorry," he says.

"For what?"

"For acting like I know better. But . . . how often do you actually get out in the field yourself?"

She rubs one of his knuckles with her thumb. This isn't professional. He works for her. But she can't help but revel in the familiar roughness of his grip. And she's glad not to go, to linger a little longer by his side. "Me? No. Never. Not ever. Nature is great, but . . . I prefer to observe it from a ski run or hiking trail. I'm just the engineer, an office drone. You're my bravehearted scouts."

"Why don't you come?" he says. "You should come."

"I don't leave pavement."

She starts to protest but he cuts her off. "Just for the plane ride. Don't you want to experience this place as more than a photo?"

"No."

"Why not?"

"Because . . ." How to respond? Because she likes things just so? Because she is afraid? There is no answer that doesn't make her feel like a neatly folded map of a place no one ever wanted to go.

"Come on." Josh lets go of her hand and it flops to her side and she feels suddenly untethered, adrift. She wobbles where she stands.

He trains his GoPro camera on her. "Okay, I'll admit it. I have a very selfish reason for wanting you to come. Every story needs a romantic interest. Who wants to watch a bunch of smelly dudes roaming around in the woods?"

She can't help but smile at this.

"Besides, aren't you the one who said it?"

"Said what?"

"There are other ways to live?"

"Did I say that?" she says and remembers that rum-drunk night long ago. "I guess I did say that."

Josh says, "Cliff? What do you think? Room for one more?"

Cliff unties the anchor ropes and approaches her, looking her up and down, making calculations in his head. "How much you weigh?"

Her smile jerks. Her eyes shift. "Um. Well . . ."

Cliff reaches out and picks her up with two hands, assessing her size. Then drops her. "Should be fine."

The plane cuts through the sky, and all around them evergreen forests reach off into an unguessable distance, dotted with lakes and fanged with mountains. Here are glaciers that seem to Michelle to give off their own special blue light. And ocean inlets are dotted with the white, surging forms of beluga whales. "Six hundred sixty-three thousand square miles," Cliff says. "You could crush Texas, California, and Montana into Alaska. The biggest state. And the least populated."

Michelle has never felt like more of a speck. The five of them are cramped into the plane. The floor and walls and ceiling are upholstered with orange shag carpet for soundproofing. A hula girl with the head of a moose is anchored to the dash.

She shouldn't be nervous. She refuses to be nervous. She has studied this area over and over and over. The maps are inside her. She tries to envision their placement from a satellite view—with the plane as a red pin—and this brings her some comfort.

Lester hands out bags of trail mix and tins of waterproof matches, and Todd says, "Thanks, Mom."

Cliff continues with his rant. He seems to view himself as some cross of tourist guide and doomsday prophet. "They call it the Ring of Fire. We're at the upper end of it. Spans a good portion of the Pacific. Volcanic hotspot. Hell on earth."

Michelle peers out the window—she's never seen so many mountains. She feels lost up here. She can't imagine how lost she would feel on the ground. Todd leans into her, so closely that his breath batters her hair. "Scared of flying? Need me to hold you comfortingly?"

"Don't be gross," she says. "But the engine on this thing does sound like five lawnmowers duct-taped together, which is not totally reassuring."

"This one time, in Ghana, we bummed a ride on an old Air America cargo plane when—"

"That's great," Michelle says and then the plane banks and steadies itself into a descent, heading toward a long lake.

"Landing here for a quick drop-off. Hunting camp called in a request. Got to re-up on ammo, whiskey, beans and rice, propane. Shouldn't take too long and we'll be on our way."

Not five minutes later, the plane skips and skims along the surface of the water, slowing and rumbling toward the lakeshore.

Everyone exits the plane and hops into the thigh-high water and helps Cliff unload and trudge the supplies toward shore, where they kick the water out of their boots and call out, "Hello?"

There is a canoe, overturned to keep the water out, and a mud-caked ATV parked on a rise. A thin wisp of smoke rises from a dead campfire. Bear bags hang from trees like cocoons, tied higher than any grizzly could reach, and YETI coolers are stacked near a wooden shelter with a stove. Three tents seem to breathe in the breeze, all of them empty.

Here is a dressing rack, made from shaved logs, where deer are hung to skin and butcher. A buck's head—with a length of spine still attached—dangles here like a terrible ornament. Flies cover it completely in a seething black mask. The ground below is muddy with blood and lumped with intestines.

A fly lands on Michelle's mouth and she spits and wipes at her lips in disgust.

"Said they'd be here . . ." Cliff turns in a slow circle. "Hello! Hey! Anybody!" His voice echoes off and then the woods claim it.

Then they hear whooping laughter and turn back to the shore and realize that they are alone. Josh and Lester and Todd have abandoned them. "What are those knucklehead friends of yours up to?"

She says, "They're my employees," and he says, "Could have fooled me, given the way you were holding hands with Prince Charming earlier."

She doesn't respond, because something has stolen her full attention. She raises an arm, pointing. First at the clothes and boots cast aside in messy piles. And then to the three young men, naked and climbing upward gingerly through the bushes, over the boulders, picking their way to the top of a basalt rise.

Here, one by one, they leap off. Howling, missiling through the thirty feet of air, and plunging into the water with a soapy splash. They swim and roughhouse, red-cheeked and exultant, and Josh waves at Michelle and in that moment danger seems so far away.

. . .

A half hour later, they're in the air again, with Cliff muscling the yoke through a rough patch of turbulence. Below, the woods give way to gray-green ocean inlets saddled between low mountains.

"Are you legitimately worried about those guys?" Josh says.

Cliff shrugs and says, "No reason to panic yet. I'll roam back here after I drop you off. But over a thousand people go missing every year in Alaska, and several hundred of them go missing right here."

Lester leans forward. "You mean the Bermuda Triangle of the North? Are we there?"

"The edge of it, yeah," Cliff says.

"I'm curious about the theories."

"*Legends* might be a better word. Some say it's ley lines." He explains the channels of energy, sometimes associated with vortexes. "Lots of ancient churches and graveyards and monuments are built around them. Technology goes haywire. Gives some people epiphanies, makes others go mad. Like a thinning between the physical and spiritual worlds. If you believe in that kind of hooey. Anyway, the places where all these ley lines converge, some people call vortexes. Some people call them doors. And some people call them trees."

"Trees?" Michelle says. "Why trees?"

"Don't know. Guess you think of the ley lines as roots. They all come together at the tree."

Lester says, "Is there any science that underpins that theory? Can you, for example, record electromagnetic anomalies in this area? Could heavy iron deposits create compass confusion that people excuse away as supernatural?"

"Maybe. Probably," Cliff says. "No matter what you believe, doesn't change the fact that this place has a way of eating people up."

They fly over a spattering of islands, what Michelle says looks like an oversize version of Puget Sound. The water throughout the inlet is curiously busy with logs. They move with the waves—the same faint, trembling motion you see in breeze-rippled reeds.

"All right," Cliff says. "This is where we say good-bye."

The plane slowly banks, making a lazy half circle of the inlet, as Cliff tries to eyeball a section of water that isn't hazardous. But the logs—the logs are everywhere. Except for one corridor of water, maybe three hundred yards long, their only option. "This will be tricky, but I can stick it." They settle into their approach, and the plane lowers until its pontoons hover just over the treetops, ready for a quick drop onto the water. "Here we go."

Just then a flock of geese explodes into view. Like dark spores driven by the wind. Their bodies strike the plane with a thud-thud-thud-thud. The windshield shatters and the wind sucks and howls into the cabin, along with a swirl of feathers, a spray of blood.

The engine sputters and whines. A propeller snaps off, flying back to knife through the tail. Their altitude drops, and they narrowly avoid the trees below, their crowns spiking the air. The plane tips one way, then another, and now they are out over the water. They can barely see, their vision wind-burned, smoke-hazed, but where there aren't logs, there are islands, and where there aren't either, the water is steely gray with waves kicking up into foamy points.

Cliff battles for control of the yoke. His eyes smear with tears from the wind. Rivulets of blood streak across his cheeks like rain on a car window.

They approach the water, the pontoons nearly touching, the plane bumping along, trying to find a hold on the water. Maybe they're going to make it after all.

A log appears on the other side of a wave, rolling toward them. It hits a pontoon, which rips off with a metallic cry. The plane lurches sideways, sheers into the cold, gray water, and kicks up a hard wave.

Everyone is thrown forward. After all that wild movement, the sudden stillness is impossible to process. Their minds remain up in the air, their bodies limp and rag-dolled by the crash.

Water seeps into the cabin in a gurgling rush. The cold stirs them, but they only have to time to cry out before their words are gargled, then silenced.

For a second, Josh believes he's back on that mountain pass with his family. The same taste of blood. The same groan of torn metal. The same brain-bruised disorientation. His family—no, his friends—will die if he doesn't do something. He needs to do something.

The plane sinks, tipping sideways, then upside down. The single pontoon maintains its buoyancy. The top of the plane strikes the muddy bottom, sending up a cloud of grit. Oil bleeds. Great wobbling bubbles rise from hidden pockets and seams.

Todd frees himself and worms through the shattered window and kicks his way to the surface.

Cliff tries to wrench open the door, but it's bent shut. Lester squeezes through the broken window and then offers a hand to Cliff and pulls. The window is too small and Cliff is too big, but there's no other way, and on the way through the frame, glass bites into him, a shard the size of a dagger lodging in his gut.

A thread of blood follows the two men as they kick their way out of sight.

Josh watches them go, still dazed. His thoughts feel tender, his body separate from him. A plastic bag—crumbed with trail mix—floats by like a jellyfish. On the other side of it is Michelle.

Her eyes are half-closed. Her skin appears as pale as alabaster. Her glasses hang crookedly on her nose, one stem broken. And her hair swirls around her face like seaweed.

A few bubbles escape Josh, the last air in his lungs. He watches them totter through the cabin and escape the window and rush to the surface. He knows he needs to follow the air if he's going to live, if he's going to save Michelle. His pulse beats in his ears, louder and louder, like a countdown to an end.

He rips loose his seat belt. And then hers, fumbling with the buckle until it clinks open. Her body flops when he curls an arm around it and tries to find a way out.

Todd stumbles out of the water and onto the shore. Of a boulder-humped and tree-studded island. He's tucked into a pocket of beach protected by a rocky point jutting out into the water. Here he hunches over, resting his hands on his knees, panting. He retches out a puddle of salt water. Then spits a few times and laughs.

His job is to microwave burritos. He sets up cameras. He posts to and monitors their social media feeds. He could maybe squeeze out a sit-up, but it's been years since he's tried. He could maybe score with a girl by swiping right, but he prefers to jerk off. He doesn't climb—he belays. He doesn't get blasted out of the cannon—he lights the fuse. He doesn't sit on the throne—he juggles and jokes. That's his role.

But damn, damn, damn, does this feel good. Like the prickling rush that follows a nut-draining orgasm or a bump of coke. No wonder Josh takes the risks that he does.

Something's been happening. Ever since they set off on this trip. He's finally felt some sense of togetherness, authorship. He's more than a prop or a grip—not just a backup singer, but a true participant.

The plane is thirty yards offshore. The pontoon juts out of the water. The current is fast, rippling along, carrying debris with it along with a rainbow slick of oil. Cliff works his way forward slowly, bobbing like a porpoise, with Lester assisting him.

"Can you believe this?" Todd calls out to them.

He doesn't notice Cliff holding his hand to his gut, the blood gloving his hand. He doesn't notice that Josh and Michelle haven't yet emerged from the wreck. Because he's buzzing so hard, every nerve lit. He can't stop the laughter rolling out of him. "Oh, shit. Oh, shit yeah! I've never rushed like that. Kiss of death. Coffin breath all over me." He lets out a whoop. He jumps up and nearly falls over, his legs wobbly. "Are you feeling what I'm feeling? Are you soaking in the same endorphin bath?"

Cliff and Lester slog out of the ocean. Lester drops to his knees and chokes out a sob. But Cliff stands there a moment, staring at Todd, before swinging a fist—the size of a brick—and knocking him flat.

Todd doesn't remember falling. He was standing up one moment, lying there the next. Dazed, barely aware of the line of blood dribbling from his nose and into his ear. All the good feeling is suddenly gone. Replaced by a dismal emptiness.

He watches some geese fly overhead, maybe from the same flock that struck their plane. They are arranged in an arrowhead formation, as if they were a weapon.

Cliff lifts his booted foot—and brings it down, hard. Onto Todd's GoPro camera. It shatters.

"Told you, didn't I?" Cliff says, several breaths between every word. "Million ways Alaska will kill you. And I'm one of them."

Lester falls to his knees in a posture of prayer. "Is it bad?"

Cliff checks his wound then, lifting his hand from his belly. The shard of glass gleams. A fresh surge of blood burbles out of it. "I'm alive. Don't know that I can say the same for the other two . . ."

He nods to the wrecked plane and the three of them all stare toward it hopelessly.

The current carries them along, and when they finally break the surface, they're past the cove. Josh's breath comes in frayed gasps. Michelle dangles off him. Her head lolls, but she's alive, coughing up water. Her broken glasses dangle from one ear, and then vanish when a wave hits them.

He doesn't know where to swim because of the logs. They roll and surge all around them, some still rough with bark, others bald and gray. They knock together with damp claps. Broken branch stems threaten to stab and claw.

One slides down a wave and torpedoes toward them—and Josh drags Michelle below. A long splinter of wood misses them by inches. He kicks hard, and then they're up again, on the other side, spitting water.

He gulps enough air to speak. "You hurt?"

She shakes her head: No? Or: She doesn't know?

He sees the island then, only twenty yards away. The current pulls them along the shore, toward the open ocean that waits at the head of the inlet. "I need you to swim hard for a little bit longer. Okay?"

Two waves converge then—each carrying a fat log—and Josh and Michelle are caught in the trough between them. "Stay with me."

He pulls her under again, as deep as he can manage, into the gray-green water, and he risks a look upward. The sunlit surface ripples and the logs scissor into place where they trod water a moment before.

When they surface, gasping, no more logs barricade the way. There is only the stone-strewn beach before them. "Come on. Almost there."

She grips his shoulders as he powers his legs and motors them toward shore. Finally they stand, the water waist-deep but the current still dragging, hard enough that they stumble and lose their balance more than once. They're soaked and shivering from the cold and adrenaline. Eventually they make it to the steep, short beach. Their shoes clatter the rocks and slip in the mud.

"Thank," Michelle says, "you."

"You okay?"

She wipes the water from her face, takes a deep, shuddering breath. Slowly spins in a circle to orient herself. He sees what she sees. Woods. Water. And logs. The mainland is a mile or so away, a forested wall. In the distance mountains rise. He knows what she must feel. Small, fragile, lost. And he knows it's wrong, but this same vulnerability makes him feel strong. He saved her. They made it out of the wreck alive. He is aware that this is a stupid metaphor—him editing the past—but it feels like exactly the stupid metaphor he needs. She might feel lost but he feels found.

"What the hell just happened, Josh?"

She stares off at the emptiness. Mosquitoes cluster around them. Whining. Needling their skin. For a moment their noise becomes the only sound. An almost electronic frequency. Michelle smacks one and screams, "Fuck! We are so fucked!" and leaves behind a bloody smear.

The satellite phone is dead. No matter how many times Lester punches the power button, no matter how hard he shakes it or says, "Come on. Come on, damn you." Nothing. Then he brings it to his mouth and closes his eyes as if he could wake it with a kiss.

He can imagine the satellites orbiting above, more than two thousand of them, listening for his signal. He can imagine the more than two hundred thousand cell towers spearing hilltops across the United States. And he can imagine the streams of data channeling between them. He recognizes, even now, the gridwork of his connection. He's not lost. He knows exactly how to get from here to there. But it's all dependent on this stupid, stupid phone.

A mewl of pain startles him and his eyes snap open.

A few minutes ago, he helped settle Cliff tenderly into a sheltered alcove, a corner of the shore walled in by basalt. Cliff sits there now with his legs flopped out and his arms wrapped around his belly as if he were hugging himself. The big man's eyes are red-rimmed and staring hard at Lester. "It's like you were saying."

Lester kneels by him. "What?" His words come out as a rasp. "What was I saying?"

"The birds," Cliff says. "It's like they didn't know where to fly. Must have been the electromagnetism that did it."

Lester tries the phone again. He knows it's ridiculous, but for a moment, he can't help but wonder if more than water damage makes it dark. "The ley lines."

"You said they must have a charge."

"It was just a guess. I don't know anything."

Cliff lifts his hands and tugs tentatively at his shirt. The blood has seeped into his jeans. He tries to pull at the glass but loses his grip, throwing back his head and stifling a cry.

"Can I do anything to help?" Lester says.

Cliff nods. "I want it out of me."

"I don't know if we should."

"I want it out."

Lester says, "Okay," and pulls down his sleeve, wrapping his hand in it, so that he has a better grip. He pinches down on the dagger of glass—and it slides out with an oozing splurt of blood.

Cliff's scream eases into a sigh as he loses consciousness. His body slackens. Something gray and purple inflates out of the wound, a distended piece of intestine.

Lester tosses the glass aside and then reaches for Cliff, as though he might tuck his guts back inside him, but his hands pause. Close enough that he can feel the heat coming off the big man's body. There's nothing to be done. "Todd?" he says.

His friend is down by the water, staring out at the plane. More of it is visible than before, due to the shifting tide. "Todd?" Lester says again, and when he gets no response, he approaches and squeezes his shoulder. "Todd . . ."

Todd looks up, only half-focused, and says, in a ghost of a voice, "They're not coming."

"No." It's hard to say the word, because it's an admission of death. His friend is dead. A part of him wants to say, I told you so, and, I knew this would happen, and, We never should have come here, but that part of him—the stage mom, his friends call it—feels like it expired in the crash as well. Worrying will do him no good out here.

"I left them behind," Todd says. "Josh wouldn't have left me."

Lester flinches as he imagines Josh and Michelle out there—their bodies gray-skinned and aquariumed by the plane—but then his focus shifts. Beyond their glazed expressions. Beyond the fish nibbling at their flesh. To the luggage at the rear of the cabin.

"That's exactly what we need," Lester says. "What we left behind."

"What do you mean?"

"The first aid kit. The water filter. Sleeping bags. Food. It's all out there." Their only hope of surviving.

"But," Todd says, his face creasing, "*they're* out there too. I can't."

"Josh always said this day was coming. You can only stick your head in the lion's mouth so many times . . ."

"He did say that. But I never believed him."

Lester holds out a hand and hoists his friend up and they stand side by side, wavering for a moment, before Lester speaks. He's surprised by the calm certainty of his voice. "The tide's going out. I'm too exhausted to fight the current. I think if we wait a little longer, we might be able hike out there. Okay?"

Todd nods until it looks like his head might fall off. "Okay."

Michelle is in charge. That's what she keeps telling herself. These are her employees. They came here because of her. She is going to get them out of here. Because she is in charge.

But the words, no matter how many times they loop through her head, won't cement into a feeling. She has no control, no confidence. Her breathing comes in fierce pants. She paces in short circles and balls her fists so tightly her nails cut into her palms.

"Let's go," Josh says, and she hates him for it. She hates him for not acting panicked or bothered in the slightest. He seems—impossibly—happy. He can't be having fun, can he? Is that the beginning of a smile curling his mouth? What once attracted her to him—his fatal glamour—now infuriates her. "Let's go," he says again.

"Where? Where are we going to go, Josh? We're trapped."

He adjusts the GoPro camera still mounted on his shoulder. "Let's go and let's find our friends."

"Stop worrying about how this is going to play online. Stop pretending. Stop acting like a hero."

"Just settle down, Michelle." He reaches out a hand. "We're going to be fine."

"Don't say that! Fear is the right response."

She ceases pacing and looks at his hand now. Not so different from the one she extended to him when he was floating in Lake Superior. She felt so confident then. Relishing the look of surprise on his face. And now? She thought she had hoisted him out of trouble—but in fact he's dragged her into it.

"My buddies might be hurt," he says, "and if so, I want to help them. I know they're worried about me. About us. Probably think we're dead. I'd like to cure them of that feeling sooner than later."

"Your friends," she says. She still won't take his hand, but allows him to step closer to her, because her mind has locked in on a realization. "Lester's got the satellite phone." At this her breathing settles completely and she neatens her ponytail and runs her hands along her sodden windbreaker as if to iron the wrinkles from it. As long as Lester has the satellite phone, they'll be fine. She'll escape this place. She'll be in her hotel by this evening, ordering room service, soaking in a hot bath, watching HGTV. Who cares if this area never gets mapped? Nature is trying to tell her something: No one should ever come here.

She speaks with a calm directive. "Let's find your friends and call the office and let them know what happened. We've gotten ourselves into some trouble, but everything's going to be fine. We're going to be okay." She ignores his hand and plunges into the woods, the gapped shadows between the trees, knowing that he'll follow, because she is in charge, dammit.

Todd doesn't want to think, doesn't want to move, doesn't want to do anything but watch Lester make a fire. The high he experienced earlier has given way to a subterranean low. He feels unplugged, out of order, blank. Sometimes he goes to this bar packed with retro games like *Pac-Man* and *Space Invaders* and *Street Fighter II*, and after a pitcher or two, he starts to get sloppy, forgets the right commands, fails to level up. TILT. That's the term gamers use. He's there now. He's tilting.

Lester doesn't ask him for help when he arranges some browned pine needles and old man's beard moss and broken branches into a short tepee. He sparks a match. The pine needles crackle. The moss smokes. He blows softly and the flame licks its way up the wood. He feeds the fire until it is waist-high. Then he strips and tells Todd to do the same. Lester wrings the water from their clothes and holds them near the flames and when they dress again they're smoke-scented.

All this time the tide pulls back, then pulls back some more, revealing barnacle-crusted rocks and clumpy wigs of seaweed. And mud. A long stretch of mud that reaches toward the plane, which is now half-visible.

"How are you feeling, buddy?" he says and Todd says, "Tilting."

When Lester says he doesn't understand, Todd says, "I know I'm supposed to feel sad, and maybe that will come later. But it's like there's no room for it. Because I'm feeling fully fucked. You know what I mean?"

Lester tells him it's time—before the tide shifts—and though Todd would prefer to stare into the nothingness of the flames, he follows his friend. They don't make it far. Their feet, and then their calves, sink and squelch into muddy, clinging pockets. Up to his knees, Todd says, "This shit is like wet concrete."

Lester pivots and slowly returns the way he came, and when Todd asks where he's going, Lester says, "I'm the idea man, aren't I? I've got an idea."

Todd tries to follow him, but can't. The mud holds him. He makes a desperate lunge for a boulder that rises out of the muck. He ends up falling, with mud up to his neck, clinging to him. With difficulty he drags himself out and says, "This is hopeless, man." Lester marches toward the woods. Before he follows, Todd wipes the mud from his arms and kicks and stomps it from his feet. "This is one hundred percent not fun, not cool."

He finds Lester before a tree—yanking at a thickly needled branch.

"What are you doing?"

"Engineering."

The branch cracks, but not cleanly. A few more hard pulls and it comes apart with a sinewy peel of bark. He tosses it to the ground.

Several branches thickly reach from the central shaft, so that it looks like a small tree in itself. He steps on top of it, tests his weight. "Can I have your boot?"

"Why?"

"I'm the smart one, remember? Do what I say."

It's reassuring to Todd, being told what to do, but Lester is normally the kindest among them. Now his expression has gone severe and his voice is clipped. "Give it to me," he says and gestures impatiently and Todd plops down and rips off his boot. Lester fingers through the mud and undoes the laces and zips them out and uses them to bind his own foot to the branch.

When he finishes, he hoists up his leg to show off what looks like a kind of snowshoe. "Understand? Help me find another in a size ten."

Now Todd gets it. He wanders among the trees, browsing for another suitable branch. But he finds something else instead.

"Lester," he says, at first quietly and then: "Lester!"

His friend sees what he sees. A face. Carved into the trunk of the tree. So that it appears like a jack-o'-lantern or scarecrow. The eyes and nose and mouth and fangs gashed into the bark, as if roughly hatcheted.

There's more than one. There's two. No, five. No, eight. A crowd of them. The monstrous totems edge the shoreline.

Todd reaches out to touch the mouth of one, and then pulls back his hand as if bitten. "What does it mean?"

"That we're not alone."

Sound hushes and light dims when Josh enters the forest, the trees rising around him like pillars in a shadowy cathedral. That's how the island feels to him, like a sacred space, holy ground. He feels—increasingly, with every minute—he has been brought here on a kind of pilgrimage. The ground is carpeted with pine needles, and his feet whisper across it.

She doesn't feel the same way. She obviously hates this place.

He can hear it in her voice and he can see it in her body, the way she stalks more than walks ahead of him, as they push through the underbrush and hurdle over logs. She swings her arms wildly at the mosquitoes that swarm them with a tremulous whine. "Remember when you said I ought to see this place as more than a picture?" She smacks another mosquito, and another. "Well, here I am—and it sucks."

What she doesn't understand is that this is good for her. He can't say that, of course. But it really is the best possible thing that could have happened. She has spent her whole life in a fluorescent-lit globe of comfort. They don't worship at the same altar. Her god blows. He's glad to see her scared.

A strange bird calls out. A two-toned whistle that Josh barely acknowledges, because Michelle has fallen to her knees. At first he thinks she's tripped—and hurries to check on her—but then he sees her kneeling by a stream and cupping her hands to pull up a drink. "Don't."

"I'm thirsty."

"You said we could die out here—and you're right. We could. If, for example, you get giardia. Death by shitting is not a good way to go. Do you agree?"

Her eyes widen. Water dribbles down her chin.

He nods upstream. "Only drink from the source of a spring."

He thinks about telling her not to worry—she's probably fine—but he likes how she falls in line beside him as they pick their way along the stream. Fifty yards later, they come to the headwater. The spring pours from a hole in the side of a short, rocky hill. The opening is a little smaller than a culvert. Something an adult could barely force themselves through.

Josh scoops a slurping drink. "It's fine." He nods for her to do the same. "Go on. It's good. It's safe."

She reaches her hands for the gushing water—and right then the water goes red. A violent red. As if they've tapped some artery in the earth. It fills her hands. Stains them. Just as she's about to take a sip. She startles and gasps and whimpers and tries to shake off the water, wipes her palms against her thighs. "Oh, Jesus, Jesus, Jesus."

And then, just as suddenly, the water goes clear again.

The sun eases toward the horizon. Shadows lengthen. Todd remains on the shore while Lester duckwalks forward, both his feet now bound to pine boughs. "Here we go," Lester says and Todd says, "You can do this, man."

Lester messily skates out onto the mud, his arms wide to keep his balance. Then he goes stiff, as if he's heard something.

"What's the matter?" Todd says. "What is it?" He glances over his shoulder at the trees—with their leering faces—as if they might have tentacled closer by their roots. He doesn't want to join Lester, but he doesn't like standing here either. The feeling of waiting and watching sickens him.

Lester digs into his pocket and holds out the phone to Todd. "You better take this. Just in case."

"Shit, you scared me. I thought . . ." But Todd isn't sure what he thought. He eases into mud up to his ankles and snatches the phone away. "You start to sink, you turn around. You hear me, Lest?"

"I hear you."

"Josh is the one who's supposed to do this kind of thing."

Lester says, "Who's the mom now?" and slops forward.

Todd lets his arms rise and fall hopelessly. "I'm just feeling like . . ." What? That this place is going to gobble them up?

Out on the mudflats, Lester waddles and shimmies forward, while on the shore, Todd checks the phone. He shakes out the water, digs some grain from the receiver, blows on the charger port. Then presses the power button. It glimmers on. "Come on, baby. Yeah, baby, baby." The home screen loads. "Hell yes."

A chime sounds. As if in response, another sound comes. From the woods behind him. A whistle. Short and high, then long and low.

He spins around and takes in the line of face-carved trees.

One is particularly frightening. It has a big black hollow at its bottom. Like a yawning mouth. Two giant, sap-crusted eyes are carved over it.

He thinks he sees—or does he?—a flutter of movement inside the hollow. He takes a few creeping steps forward and squints his eyes to focus better and tucks the phone into his pocket. He steps closer. Then closer still. The darkness of the hollow is grave, as if some section of the night has been carved away and stored here.

He crouches down toward the tree. And then—in a blurred frenzy—he is dragged into the tree. Into the hole. Gone.

Lester closes in on the plane, now splashing through puddles of water. The mud is looser out here, more mucusy. A funk comes off it. His thighs burn. He breathes heavily from the exertion. He squints at the half-sunken plane—the windows splintered and mucked over—worried about what he might find inside.

If he were to look closer, maybe he'd see the reflection of the shore behind him. The movement there would be hazy, indistinct, but he would be able to tell that something was coming. People? Or wraiths? Or beasts? Three of them? Five? Emerging from the shadows of the forest and starting down the rocky beach. They approach the alcove where Cliff rests. They could be anyone. Or anything.

But Lester doesn't know this, just as he doesn't know that Cliff's eyes are half-lidded with nausea and exhaustion, that he's alive and awake, but barely able to lift his head at their approach. Lester doesn't know that when their shadows fall over the big man, his face goes through a series of quick transformations, ranging from hopeless pain to muddled confusion to bald fear.

Something slashes at him then. A blurred claw. Or skeletal hand. It's impossible to make sense of except as a threat. Three gashes open on Cliff's face, his cheek unzipped, one of his eyes suddenly slit.

No, Lester doesn't see any of this, but he hears the scream— and tries to twist around. "Todd? Cliff?" But his bound feet are entrenched in the mud and he loses his balance and one of the branches snaps beneath him. The loose foot instantly sinks, and he collapses onto his side. "Help!" he says as the mud sucks at him, lipping him greedily. He flounders, trying to stay upright, and the other foot comes loose from its purchase. He sags lower and lower, past his knees, his waist, up to his chest. "Help!"

He throws out his arms out as if to tread water. The mud bubbles and plops and slurps. "Help," he says. "Please!"

Then something splats nearby. Close enough that he can see the crater. He's barely able to process this—a rock, someone has thrown a rock—when another whizzes past his ear. Then another, another, another, dimpling the mud all around him. He can't see anything. He's too low. And sweat and grime bother his vision. But he can feel the rock that strikes his cheek. A flap of skin opens and throbs. His mouth tries to form around a word, but fails, and he screams instead.

He continues to sink as the stones hail all around him. One strikes the elbow of his pleading arm. Another his knuckle. Another his collarbone. He is struck in the shoulder, the ear, the eyebrow.

Sometimes the rocks come in quick succession. Other times they are interrupted by a long wait, as if someone is cruising the shore for the perfect grenade.

Lester's face is angled toward the sky and the mud tugs at his jaw and he focuses on an osprey overhead. It pounds its wings, carrying a fish that struggles in its talons.

The air purples, a twilight gloom. Michelle looks over her shoulder constantly as she and Josh tromp through the woods but stay close to the shore. Every tree seems to reach for them with its branches, to claw and grab. She swats at mosquitoes with an almost syncopated beat. They cloud around her but seem to ignore Josh.

He keeps telling her not to worry, but then she sees him crack a thick dead branch off a tree. He tests its weight and swings it like a club—then uses it as a walking stick. He gives her a just-in-case look. So Michelle grabs a stick of her own. Maybe he is scared after all. Maybe he's just better at swallowing it down.

"Iron can stain water red," he says. "There might be iron deposits here."

"That was blood, Josh." She doesn't say it, but she thinks it: It was as if the island was bleeding.

"We need to stay calm."

"Bullshit." She swings the stick—to smack him—and he holds up his own, and they clack together. "What's wrong with you? This isn't a YouTube stunt. There's no bungee cord to stop us when we fall. Be crazy!" She swings her stick again and again, and he blocks her each time. "There's a part of you that's enjoying this." He gives up on defending himself against her, and her stick prods him right in the chest, over the heart. "Admit it. You're enjoying this?"

She pushes hard with the stick, and it shoves him back, and he follows the momentum, hiking away from her. That's how they belong. Separate from each other. He likes dirt and she likes to get rid of it. She likes things zipped up and double-knotted and he likes to let it all hang out.

The feeling seems to be mutual. He curses as he shoves aside a branch, kicks through some ferns. She waits a moment, not really wanting to follow, but knowing she has no choice. She passes a wide-waisted tree—with a hollow in it the size of a dinner plate—and she feels a puff of cold air come from it, as if it were breathing. Maybe she would see a dark shape hidden within the hole, if only she looked a little closer.

Instead she hurries to catch up with him and says, "Wait."

"You promise to lay off."

"I promise to try."

She catches up with him on a knobby rise. He points and she can see the shoreline through the trees. "Think we're getting close."

"That spit of rock up ahead," she says. "We swept past it when we first came up."

She hears a strange sound then. A birdy chatter. A clacking of beaks. A rustling of wings. "Do you . . . ," she says and he says, "What?" "Sh."

They look around curiously. Bright red berries grow on a bush. A slug oozes along and its eyestalks rise from its head like horns. And then they hear more of it. A clacking and rustling and hissing and garbled honking, a sound that makes no sense.

They push through a thicket—and look up. Here is a massive wooden cage. Built high between two trees and bound together by ligaments. It is crammed with geese. Maybe thirty of them. They flap their wings and claw their feet and hiss with their thin pink tongues out. They bite one another, snatching out clumps of feathers that snow down.

"I don't . . . ," she says, but never finishes.

The plane. Just like what hit the plane. She backs up—shaking her head no—with an ugly calculation whirring through her head. "Someone put them there. That means someone let them loose."

"That doesn't make sense," he says. "That's impossible."

She backs up, and her foot catches against something. What at first appears to be a root. But it stretches and lifts and rattles. A chain.

She nearly falls but catches herself. And then looks up to see where the chain leads.

To a wolf. The color of charcoal. Fifteen feet away. In the shade its eyes are the bright gold of candle-flames. It wears a collar. Linked to the chain. Linked to a tree.

The wolf lowers its triangular head. Its back bunches into a hump. Its muzzle wrinkles and reveals the needled teeth nested in candy-slick gums. A growl boils out of it, shivering the air. Its hindquarters tense—and it surges forward.

"Run!" she says, and together they sprint away from the wolf.

It closes the distance quickly and leaps, its jaws widening. In the air, its leash catches, the chain at its end. And the snarl is caught short and gives way to a yip.

The wolf falls. Then immediately springs up again. Testing the length of its chain, straining against its collar, and clacking its teeth.

There is a moment—a brief moment—when Michelle and Josh clutch each other and think they're safe. But then a rattle comes from behind them.

They spin around to see another wolf charging toward them. They trip over stumps and nudge into each other and duck beneath branches as they race away. Changing direction, again and again, as wolf after wolf leaps after them.

Just as one is caught short by its leash, another appears. It is a gauntlet. Every wolf has its own territory—the radius of its chain—with none intruding upon the other. They make a terrible noise, all of them barking and yowling together.

Whether this is a trap or some elemental alarm system, Josh and Michelle don't know. But they're nearly bitten twenty different times, jaws snapping shut inches from their hands, their ankles, their necks. Spittle flecks them.

Josh knocks a white wolf back with his walking stick. Michelle spins on one foot, a clumsy kind of pirouette, to avoid another wolf with an eye scarred shut. In this way, they stutteringly progress through the woods.

Then a wolf with a narrow face nicks Josh's leg—and tugs and tears his pants. He falls just out of its reach, and it snarls and grinds at its chain. His calf bleeds, a chunk torn out of it. Perhaps she's imagining it, but she thinks his voice might shake when he speaks: "Maybe there's a tribe here. Or maybe they're survivalists. Maybe they can help."

"No one is supposed to live here. This is the edge of the middle of nowhere. And are you not seeing what I'm seeing? A logjam to keep planes from landing. Goose cages and wolf traps? Whoever's here is not interested in helping anyone."

Still he doesn't look afraid. He looks upset and determined and a bit crazed when he brings his hands to either side of his mouth and cries out, "Hello?"

"I don't think that's a good idea."

"Is anybody there?"

"Stop. Josh. No."

He waits another long beat before chucking his walking stick in frustration. It spears the air and stabs a cluster of ferns. There is a sharp cry and someone springs up. A girl with long hair decorated with burrs and fir needles. Maybe ten years old. She bounds away from them. And while Michelle knows it makes no sense, she can't help but think: I know her—that's me.

Josh grew up in the suburbs of Beaverton, but his parents always wanted another life. They tilled their lawn and replaced it with apple trees and raised vegetable beds. They anchored solar panels to the roof and posted a wind turbine in the backyard. They built a chicken coop and installed bee boxes. His father harvested most of their meat, and the neighbors would sometimes complain when he hung a deer from the maple in the front yard to skin and butcher.

His mother made their clothes. Their basement was shelved with the pickled beets and applesauce and salsa and jams and spaghetti sauce she canned. She read her way through the Foxfire books and compared what she learned in them to advice on online forums about sustainable living. She took notes on the same yellow legal tablets Josh's father used in court. He was maybe the only defense attorney in Portland who grew a beard halfway down his chest and drove a rusted Dodge pickup with a retooled engine that ran on french fry grease.

Josh and his sister, May, enjoyed the weekend trips—hiking and hunting and fishing in the Cascades—but they complained endlessly about their parents' lifestyle choices. They wanted to eat a McDonald's cheeseburger every now and then, for God's sake. Their clothes were embarrassingly free of logos. Why couldn't they own a television and a computer and a phone like everyone else? Who cared if antiperspirant had carcinogens in it—they'd rather have cancer than stink.

Then came the decision to quit it all. That was the phrase his parents used. "Let's quit it all and get back to basics." They bought a hundred acres in eastern Oregon—in the foothills of the Ochoco Mountains. His father would retire from his law practice. His mother would homeschool the kids. They would live in a yurt while the cabin was under construction. They didn't consider themselves survivalists, but off-gridders, back-to-the-landers.

"No," Josh told them. "Just no." His parents were making a selfish decision. They couldn't steal his life from him. What about his friends? His hopes for college? It was another year before he graduated from high school. Seven for his sister. Couldn't they wait? They had a weird life now, but this would destroy any semblance of normalcy. His aunt Libby lived in Portland and he begged to move in with her. "I cannot do this," Josh told them. "I would rather die."

He got his wish. They were on their way to the property—Oasis, they nicknamed it—when they spun out and crashed through the railing and spiraled down the embankment. May was eleven when she died.

And now—but it can't be?—now his sister is running ahead of him. With the same long, dirty-blond hair. In the same stupid homemade clothes she had been wearing that day. Brown corduroys and a green T-shirt, only dirt-stained, split-edged. Like something that had been buried and dug up years later. He knows it's impossible, but he chases her anyway. "Wait!"

The girl wears a mask. A deer skull with two short horns has been fitted over her head with leather straps.

The bite in his calf throbs. Bushes scratch his legs and tree branches swat his face and boulders and logs trip his feet. But the girl races through it all without pause. A blur, a phantom riding the wind. He can't keep up with her—and Michelle can't keep up with him. For a time he can hear her calling after him, but then her voice ghosts away.

"Stop!" he yells, his chest burning with the hot wind of his breath. "Please! I promise not to hurt you."

Finally, against a thick cluster of cedars, the girl spins around, and he skids to a stop, only a few yards away. He can barely make out the eyes inside the girl's mask. Are they blue? They look blue.

It's her. It's May. He can't quite bring himself to say her name. And now that he's caught up to her, he doesn't seem to know what to do. He pats his pockets until he finds what he's looking for. "Here." He pulls out a Ziploc bag. "You want some trail mix?"

He rips open the bag, scoops out an M&M, pops it in his mouth. "I only eat the rest of this junk to get to the chocolate." He offers the bag to her—and when she doesn't take it, he tosses it her way. With one hand she snatches it from the air.

"It's good," Josh says, the sweetness still in his mouth. "Try it."

A stick snaps behind him, and he turns, expecting Michelle. But it's not. There is only the woods. And when he returns his attention to the girl, she, too, is absent. No branches sway where she passed by. No moss sponges upward, freed from her weight. It was as though she was never there.

"Dammit." He tromps around, circling trees, peering into a cavitied log, stomping through ferns. "She was here." He swipes a hand through the air, as if the cobwebs of her might linger, something to catch with his fingers. "She was right here."

Michelle isn't a runner. She prefers yoga and a brisk daily walk. When Josh goes tearing off into the woods after the girl, she does her best to keep up with them. But the trees are so thick and the ground slopes and is tangled with brush. It doesn't take long for her to lose sight of him. She leans against a tree and the bark roughs her cheek. "Josh," she says, knowing he won't hear her. But his name makes her feel a little less alone.

She takes in her surroundings. The canopy is thick and even at noon only a few blades of sunlight could knife through. Now it's evening, and darkness smokes the air. A hill rises nearby, banded with rock. She can see a clearing of bear grass not far away. A beetle scuttles across a log. A conk fungus bulges from a stump. A long line of ants stitches the forest floor, one of them lumbering under a leaf ten times its size. She follows their direction and sees something. Something she can't quite make sense of. Her chin trembles. Her hand settles over her heart.

She pushes through a bony tangle of manzanita bushes and finds herself looking around, in wonder, at what might ordinarily pass for a junkyard. But not here. Here it's a graveyard. She is surrounded by dozens of wrecked boats and planes. Some old and quilled with pine needles and mudded with wasp nests. Others are newer. Their hulls are broken. Their wings are snapped. Metal weeps rust. Cracks zigzag through plastic. And the farther she walks, the older the equipment. The more vine-tangled and dirt-buried.

Michelle's hand lingers on a canoe with a Rorschach test of rust or blood staining it. There are others. Who have come here and never left. And now she is among them.

In the center of it all, there is a tree. Or *the* tree. The biggest she has ever seen outside of the sequoias. She has to crane her neck to the limit to take it all in. The bark is gray and rough and plated like an elephant's skin. Scored through by lightning strikes. Burled and hollowed, so that it appears to be knuckled and jointed and eyed and mouthed many times over. Its branches, some bald and some thickly needled, could be a forest of their own.

She can feel a panic rising in her. A knee-jellying, lung-deadening panic. But it stills suddenly, as if a valve has turned, when she notices something impossible. On that same tree. Amid the thick tangle of roots. The scales of bark stitch together into the shape of a door. And not just any door. But a white, six-panel slab with a gold handle. With a map of the world tacked to it.

Her door. The entrance to her childhood room. The closer she comes, the more perfect and crystalline the illusion grows, solidifying before her.

A part of her wants to run in the opposite direction, screaming. But another part of her feels comforted by the promise of what waits inside. She reaches for the handle.

· · ·

Josh bursts out of the woods onto the rocky beach and slides to a stop and crouches with his hands fisted. All the way here, he ran, certain something was right behind him. Or above him. Or even below him. Just certainly near, its fungal breath in his ear.

But nothing pursues him. His eyes dart between the trees—with the terrible faces carved into them—as they sway and whisper in the wind. "Todd?" he says after a long few seconds. "Lester?" He can feel his pulse in his bitten calf.

The sun has retreated to a red line on the horizon. The last of its light burnishes the wing of the plane, half-sunken in the mud. The tide is starting to roll in, creeping into the inlet with a lapping froth. This is the place. He saw his friends swim free of the plane and this is where they must have come to shore. But the beach is empty. "Cliff?" he says, his voice skipping off across the water. "Guys! Yo! Where are you?"

Then he catches a whiff of smoke. Wisps rise from a dying fire in an alcove. He approaches slowly. "Michelle?"

Here is a giant pile of stones. A cairn, he realizes. Like the ones he builds before every stunt. But this one is nearly as tall as him, a kind of pyramid. And a boot is visible at its base. Stained, salt-rimed leather, square-toed, maybe a size fourteen.

Josh begins to remove the rocks. Hesitantly at first, then faster, shoving and clawing them away. They bruise his shins and clatter around his feet. He knows what's inside, but he still looks away when he confirms it. Not wanting to believe what he sees.

Cliff's hair is full of dirt. A few rocks still balance along his shoulder and bury his arm, but Josh can see that his belly has been sliced open like a smile. A mass of pebble-specked innards bulges out of him. Three red lines track diagonally across his face. From a knife? A pitchfork? A claw? Before Josh can process what he's discovered, a tiny voice calls out, "Help."

At first it seems like Cliff is talking, though his mouth doesn't move. "Josh," the voice says, his name spoken so quietly, it's barely noticeable. "Please." He spins in a circle, hunting for the source.

"Lester?"

"Please."

"Lester! Lester, where are you?"

Out on the mudflats. Josh follows the messy tracks that lead to the plane. His body has sunk into a sloppy crater. He lies flat on his back, his head buried up to his ears. A single hand motions to Josh, the fingers weakly trembling.

Josh scrambles to the top of the alcove for a better view. In the failing light, it's hard to see, but he can make out his friend—the oval of his face—but he appears cut and swollen. Only one of his eyes is open, the other a purpled mound. "Josh," Lester says. "Here."

At that very moment the tide rolls in and covers him with a gurgling wave.

Lester has always been good at math. Calculating the SCR of a scuba dive, the speed at which to hit a ramp, the tax deductions when filing as a corporation. He doesn't have to force his mind to see the numbers: they're always there, announcing themselves. A shaft of sunlight falls at a sixty-degree angle, a stoplight takes three seconds to go from yellow to red, it will take him two and half miles at a four-miles-per-hour pace to burn off the 563-calorie Big Mac he ate. That kind of thing.

So he's been carefully listening to the water's approach, as it rolls forward and pulls back, steadily closing in on him. He believes that when it finally hits, he'll have to hold his breath for thirty seconds. He's not in the best shape, but he knows he can go sixty seconds or more without feeling strained.

The roaring coldness of the water surprises him. His left ear feels stabbed by the force of it. It worms up his nose and seeps into his mouth and threatens to make him gag and cough. His neck pops. The mud moves around him, readjusting with the current, pulling him down an inch farther, maybe more.

How Josh survived, he doesn't know. Maybe he's hallucinating. Or maybe they all died in the plane crash and this is some kind of hell and a ghost is taunting him from the shore. He can't see anything—except a grainy swirl—and he can't hear anything beyond the rumbling hush. It reminds him of static. Of a television caught between stations. And a memory comes rushing to the fore of his mind.

He was a boy who built things. Model planes. Tube radios. A lamp. Even a television from salvaged parts. His bedroom was a mess of wires and circuit boards and soldering irons and spice jars packed with screws and nails and washers. His older brother, Ike, wasn't like him. He was wasp-waisted and broad-backed with interests that didn't seem to extend beyond girls and the ball field. He called Lester a robot-loving faggot. He shouldered past him in the hallway, knocked his cereal bowl from his hands, dropped his toothbrush in the toilet. And that day—the day of the static—he took a baseball bat to the television set Lester had spent over a month building. He cracked the screen, snapped a leg, bent the antenna. The caveman cartoon that had played perfectly a moment before warped and fuzzed over and gave way to ghosts. Lester cried out, "Why would you do that? Why do you hate me so much?"

This was not the worst thing his brother ever did to him. Not even close. But it felt like the beginning of the worst. And that part of his brain felt as busted-up and short-circuited as that home-brewed television.

Josh looked like he came from a similar mold as Lester's brother—hard eyes, square chin, a body like a weapon—but they couldn't be more different. Josh didn't want to hurt anyone but himself. He would rescue Lester from this. He imagines his friend trying to rush out onto the mud and instantly failing as it glops around his ankles and calves. He imagines him looking around stupidly, trying to figure out what to do. He won't have time to cobble together and tie on a set of makeshift snowshoes, like Lester, so he'll have to find another way.

A log. That's what Josh will do. The shore is busy with logs and he'll heft one up—as wide as his leg, twice as tall as him—and raise it up like a totem, before letting it fall into the mud with a splurt. And it will bridge the way out.

There—the water is pulling back now. The sound of static retreats. Mud slugs his cheek and grit seethes through his hair. And he is spitting and sputtering for breath, blinking away the salt that stings his eyes.

Surely Josh is almost there. He can hear his voice—can't he? Yelling, I'm coming, buddy! If only his ears weren't plugged with mud. One log won't get Josh here. He'll have to gather and arrange several, along with some chunks of driftwood that might serve as unstable bedding for him to clamber across. It will be inadequate, unsafe, but he's desperate. He'll do it, tightroping his way there.

Lester is about to scream for help, when the tide hits him again, a smothering liquid blanket. The static, the static—it's in his ears and eyes now. It's all around him, a fizzy nothing. He is a lost signal, a blank screen, a broken television.

He isn't ready, and this time it will be longer, forty-five seconds, maybe a minute, maybe more. He didn't gather enough breath to make it that long. All the calculations in the world won't help him out here. Nature is looser and meaner than math.

Already his lips tremble and his throat spasms as he tries to keep his body shut down, clamped up. He shouldn't move—that only makes him sink farther—but he can't help himself. He throws up an arm—his fingers reaching through the water and making one last weak grab for the air, as if he might pull down a breath with him.

That's when he feels Josh's hand snatch his. Clamping and shifting his wet grip. Yanking him, struggling him upward, against the foaming surf. A little at a time, until his head surfaces, finally free. He breathes in water and coughs it back out, his lungs hitching. The tide has pulled away now, but Lester is barely aware, with only one salt-burned eye capable of seeing. His body is socked with mud and cold to the core. He knows he shouldn't reach so desperately for

Josh—and risk dragging him down—but he can't stop himself. All the numbers have scrambled in his head. He is certain of nothing except his need to breathe.

His shoulders come loose—then his belly, his waist, a long, horrible birth. His ears might be plugged, but he can still hear Josh's muffled voice saying, "I've got you, friend."

Weakly, they crawl across the uncertain bridge Josh built. Lester can't stop coughing, but he manages to patch together a sentence. "Thought. You. Were. Dead."

"I'm unkillable, remember? An unkillable bastard. Isn't that what you called me once?"

Lester barks more than laughs, and then the tide turns again, chasing after them. The water finds them on a log, frothing over it, claiming their wrists and knees, and Josh coaches him forward, saying, "Almost there," and "You can do this," and "You're safe now."

That's where he's wrong. There's nothing safe about the shore. But Lester can't respond except to say, "They, they, they, they." As in, *they* got Cliff and Todd. And *they* tried to stone him. And *they* left him to drown. And *they* might be watching right now.

"Who?" Josh says, pulling him out of the final stretch of water. "Who's *they*, Lester?"

For a second, Lester almost says, My brother.

Todd can't open his eyes. Dried blood binds his eyelashes. He can't remember how, but he gashed his head. His brain feels bruised, every thought failing before it can take form. How long he's been out, he doesn't know. Where he is, he doesn't know, but it smells like earthworms and he can hear a muffled dripping, so his first thought is, Basement. He's in a basement. Underground.

He slips in and out of consciousness a few more times before waking fully. Then he takes in a big, panicked breath as a rush of images comes at him. The camera packs. The plane. The island. The trees with faces carved into them.

He tries to reach a hand to his wound, but can't. He's tied down.

His wrists. Ankles too. His body arranged upright in a chair. It takes many minutes, but he finally blinks his crusted eyes free.

The chair is made of antlers. The walls are cut from dirt and stone. Roots dangle like hair from the ceiling. The space is dim, but oranged by some light. His eyes settle wildly on something. A man wearing a bone mask. Long-snouted, with fangs as big as fingers. A bear. Along his wrist he wears a three-pronged antler braceleted by a leather strap, so that its horns appear like a claw. His clothes are stitched from furs. His hair is long and clumped. Beside him is another wearing a wolf skull, a long beard mossing his chest. A woman in a deer skull, with feathers braiding her hair. And a man wearing a whale skull. A small one, what must be a baby's, but the mouth is long and strange and reaches to his waist like an awful bill.

Todd doesn't realize he is screaming until he runs out of breath. When he does, they all lean toward him and begin screaming themselves. Mocking him. Assaulting him with voices that come together into a single rough-throated cry.

He scrunches his eyes shut, trying to hold on to the darkness and wishing everyone away, and just like that, their voices go silent. No, everything goes silent. He has no sense of up or down or left or right. Maybe he passed out again, but he might as well be floating through space. Then—every sense seems to whisper slowly into existence.

First he feels sunlight on his skin and traffic from a nearby highway and the buzz of an electric meter. He smells the cat piss stink of weed and the tang of summer-heated blacktop. When his eyes snap open, he knows instantly where he is. Behind his high school, next to the dumpster. He pinches a joint between his fingers, and a girl stands before him, opening and closing her hand in a gimme motion. Her blond hair is cut short and spiked with gel. She wears purple Doc Martens and acid-washed denim shorts and a Misfits T-shirt two sizes too big. Suzie Neighbors. He hands her the joint and she sucks a lungful off it. "Sorry," she says and a cloud of smoke hits him and makes his eyes water. "But we're done." He asks her why, but he already knows the answer, already knows she'll say it after she flicks the joint at him and stalks away. "Because you're a loser, Todd."

He blinks and the scene shifts. He's standing on a bartop in Jamaica. A crowd of people has gathered around, laughing and clapping. He wears no pants, but something dangles from his ass. A wad of toilet paper that trails thirty squares or so down the bar. Josh sparks a match and lights the tip and the fire licks its way forward and he bends his knees and kicks his feet, the dance of the flaming asshole, while everyone chants his name.

Todd blinks and now he's in his parents' living room. He sits on the couch, while his mother and father stand before him. The sun is at such an angle—coming through the picture window—that he has to squint to see them, their figures dark and casting long-limbed shadows across the floor. They have his report card in hand. They're telling him he'll never make it into college, never make anything of himself. He's a fool. He's a clown. He's a follower. Todd tries to tell them about his plans. He and Josh and Lester—they're planning on launching this channel. This YouTube channel, and—but he never finishes, because his father tears the piece of paper in half, and then in half again, and hurls the confetti of it at him.

Todd blinks—and his friends stand before him. Back in the strange room cut out of the earth with roots stringing the ceiling. Josh and Lester. Cliff and Michelle. They're all here. They're all alive. They smile kindly, and he smiles, too, even when he tries to stand and realizes he can't. Because he remains chaired in place.

Josh steps forward. He has an antler lashed to his wrist. The three horns of it are sharpened and gleam whitely. It jabs forward—and Todd cries out, "No!"—before he realizes that Josh is freeing him, slicing through the bindings that anchor his wrists and ankles.

Todd looks around wonderingly. He rubs the reddened skin. And stands. Part of him wants to run toward his friends and pull them into a hug. But another part of him wants to rush away from here. Their smiles seem too big now, with too many teeth crammed inside them. "Dance for us," Josh says.

Todd mouths the word *What?* but can't quite say it.

This time they all say it together: "Dance for us, fool."

Todd shakes his head no. When he backs away, the smiles grow wider still, reaching all the way to their ears. Many hands reach for him and push and pull him. "Dance for us," they say. "Fool, fool, fool."

The walls are yellow where they're not papered with maps. The curtains are pulled aside to reveal a brilliant summer day, and Michelle kneels in a square of sunlight now, playing with her bears. She's gathered a collection of them over the past two years, and they're her favorite toys. Plastic figurines that come with costumes and props. The sister bear has long red fur that can be combed and styled. The papa bear comes with a hat collection. The bears drive cars and the bears cook meals and the bears celebrate Christmas.

Right now the bears are on an adventure, ranging around the woods, searching for the best place to have a picnic. She has laid down a National Forests map for imaginative effect, and nudges the bears across the topographic features as they discuss the benefits of a coulee over a mountaintop for their meal.

In her excitement, her hand moves too swiftly and knocks one of the bears to the side. The brother bear. He tumbles across the floor and comes to a rest near the heat register and her narration of the picnic adventure ends. She's trying to remember something, but it escapes her. Like a dream that still flickers around the edges of your mind as you're brushing your teeth, changing out of your pajamas.

She leans toward the register and feels a warm wind breathing out of it. The metal venting drops down six inches and then elbows off into darkness. Down there she can see a thick layering of dust and a dead moth.

She is about to return to her map when she remembers. She was playing just like this—in her room, with her bears—when a voice came trembling through the grate. It was her older brother, Zack, whose room was below hers. He said he could hear her and she said, "So?" and he said, "It's annoying."

"Then stop listening."

She resumed playing for another minute, and then he called up, "Hey, I've got a fun idea."

"What?"

He told her to drop something down the register. A pencil or a ball or something.

"Why?"

"Because I think it will drop into my room. I think I can catch it."

"Okay," she said and found a cupcake-shaped eraser and pulled off the grate and said, "Here it comes," and dropped it and it slid and bumped down the vent pipe. "Did you get it?"

"Got it!" he said. "Now do one of your bears."

"No way."

"Do it. Then we can play with them down here together."

"Really?"

"Sure."

So she dropped them. One after the other. Sister, papa, and all the rest. Her favorite toys. They vanished, sliding off into the dusty, dark guts of the house. When she ran downstairs, she found her brother lying on his bed, his hands tucked behind his head, a small smile on his face. "What?" he said.

"Where are the bears?" she said.

"I don't know," he said. "You're the one who dropped them down the vent."

She had never cried harder or longer in her life. Not even when her grandmother or dog died. And she had never felt so much anger at someone, but also a sense of self-condemnation. It was her fault because she had trusted him. She made a promise—an eight-year-old's promise, but still, the mark of it lasted all these years—that she would never trust anyone.

Never trust anyone. It would be easier, so much easier, if she could, but she can't. She can't trust her toys, so she can't trust the room, so she can't trust the dreamscape she's lost in. She brings her hands to the side of her head as if to contain her thoughts. She stands and reels before the wall. The wall of maps. Here is the collage of the globe, the country, the state, the city—each with an X on it. An X that implies *You are here.* She is there.

No—she is not. And it's then that the illusion begins to crack through and she can feel her mind beating at it until it nearly shatters. "It's not real," she says and lashes out, punches a hand into a map and through the wall itself. She swipes again and tears down a map of the country and kicks the baseboard and slams her shoulder against the drywall. There is a puff of dust, the splintery crunch of the rotten studs beneath, and then it all comes crumbling down around her.

And she finds herself instead in an earthen tunnel.

"I should have waited for her," Josh says.

Night has fallen. The stars that speckle the darkness seem outnumbered only by the trees in the forest. A campfire crackles on the beach, far from Cliff's body, and by the orange glow of it Josh helps Lester clean away the mud and examine his wounds. "She called after me. She told me to stop. But I wasn't thinking. I was chasing—"

What exactly? The ghost of his sister? Or some child who—impossibly—lived here? The daughter of whomever Lester thought he saw on the shore? It's easier not to ask questions. It's better not to think at all. That's always been true for him. He's always better off when he has a mission, some pressing task to fulfill. Whether it's wing-suiting off a skyscraper or escaping the plane or saving Lester, when his mind is singularly focused, it doesn't wander in dizzying circles as it does now.

"Maybe she's fine," Lester says. "Maybe Todd's fine too." But there's nothing in his voice worth believing.

Lester was talking earlier about ley lines and energy vortexes. Compass points spinning and radio signals scrambling. But really, it's Josh's mind that feels like it's short-circuited. If he listens to the slop of the tide, to the wheeze of the wind, he hears something. Something beckoning. Something that's been waiting for him. It has a terrible secret that will make moss fur his tongue and flowers spring from his eyes and roots reach out from beneath his toenails.

"Josh!" Lester says and the world snaps back into focus.

"What?"

"You went someplace else."

"Sorry."

"I was trying to tell you about the phone." He studies Josh with his one good eye, while touching the other one tenderly, the pouched-over bruise sealing his vision. "I gave it to Todd before I tried for the plane."

Josh rubs both hands across his face and blows a sigh through the fingers. "Where we are isn't a secret, right? Someone will come for us." His breath is soured with spent adrenaline.

"But when?"

"When they realize Michelle's missing. Or Cliff's missing."

"She never told anyone she was coming—remember? Atlas doesn't know she's here. And that plane will be lost to the mud sooner than later."

Josh closes his eyes for a long time and readjusts his expectations. "You said you thought they took Todd. Where?"

Lester sweeps his arm, as if to say: The island, the night, who the hell knows.

Then comes a sound. From behind them. Among the trees. A skitter of rocks.

They go silent and stare into the impenetrable black for a minute. Then Josh picks up a stick wigged with lichen. He jabs it into the fire until the flame catches and uses it as a torch when approaching the scar-faced trees.

The inexact light makes their carved mouths appear to move, as if they are cackling silently. He limps up and down the line of them—the bite in his calf aching—and then pauses before the hollow tree. Something glints at its base. He kneels, reaching out a hand to pluck a red M&M from the ground. He clenches it in his palm a moment, so that when he opens it again, the candy has melted and smeared.

The stick has burned down enough that he hurls it back to the beach. Lester digs into his pocket and clicks on a penlight that projects a thin yellow funnel. "This will work better."

"He's in there," Josh says.

"In there?"

"Down there. Below."

"How do you know?"

He pops the M&M in his mouth and crunches down. "I know."

Lester trains the penlight on the tree, illuminating the ground before the hollow. The dirt here is as glossy as a frequently used trailhead. The hollow appears to be a rough doorway that drops into a stone staircase.

A few peanuts and crumbles of Chex mix dot the steps and Lester says, "You're suggesting we follow the breadcrumbs into the enchanted forest?"

"That's exactly what I'm saying."

"Those stories usually have a witch in them, Josh."

"Do you have another suggestion?"

Lester takes a long time to answer. "Part of me is like, what if it's a trap?" he says with a sigh. "But then I guess nothing's changed, since we've been in the trap ever since the plane crashed."

"I'm going," Josh says.

"Then I'm coming. Nobody's leaving anyone behind in the dark."

Josh doesn't tell Lester about the need that animates him. Need beyond any thought. Need as a feeling. A brain stem firing to nerve endings, the raw ingredients of himself. The need compels him to go down. He has his mission. He knows what he needs to do. To join the girl below. May. He knows that's where she's hiding. And if she's there, maybe all the rest of them are too. His mother and father. As if the island were an open grave, and he's discovered the entrance.

They travel down, hunching over so as not to bash their heads. They brace their hands against the walls and follow the curling staircase through thick stripes of earth—a loamy brown, a granular yellow, and then some clay that has the red quality of muscle, all of it veined thickly with roots. And then the floor bottoms out and a tunnel stretches before them.

The space is wide enough for two people to walk abreast. Tall enough that they shouldn't have to duck their heads, but the claustrophobia of the place makes them curl and clench their bodies. Into the walls—intermittently, at random heights and distances—there are hollows with animal skulls tucked into them.

Timber supports buttress the tunnel. From one of these dangles a lit lantern. On the floor beneath it is a rusty tank sloshed full of kerosene.

"Are they survivalists?"

"I don't think that's the right word for what we're seeing."

"Then what is?"

Lester says, "There's something—I don't know—almost ceremonial about this place. The trees and the cairn. The skulls arranged here. If it's supposed to be this confluence of ley lines . . . maybe somebody's treating it like a church."

"Like a cult?"

When he speaks again, it's barely perceptible. "Or a coven."

Josh looks over Lester's shoulder—and just past the lantern's light, where the shadows take over, he sees his parents. His father has sawdust in his beard. His mother is drying her hands on a dish towel. They look at each other and then at him, opening their arms, inviting him into a hug.

"Josh?" Lester says and snaps his fingers. "Josh!"

The vision of them swirls away, into the depths of the tunnel, like paint down a drain. Josh starts to chase after them but Lester holds up a hand to stop him. "What's wrong with you?"

"Thought I saw something."

"What?"

Josh doesn't tell Lester what he saw or that even now he hears voices whispering just out of earshot.

"Josh?"

"Forget it."

"You're not alone, you know," Lester says.

"I know."

"I mean I've seen things too."

"For real?" Josh says.

"I don't know if anything's *for real* . . . but yes."

Neither of them chooses to elaborate, but Josh finally says, "It's been a long time since I felt scared. But I think I'm there now."

"That's good," Lester says. "It's good to be scared." He pulls the lantern off the hook. "Just remember I can smell the kerosene burning in this lantern. I can wrap my hand around its metal handle. The same person who hung it from that hook dug these tunnels and threw those rocks and built that trap full of geese and chained up those wolves." Lester puts a hand on his shoulder, and squeezes hard, a demand that Josh stay with him. "We might have fallen off the map, but the laws of gravity still apply."

Michelle moles her way blindly through the tunnel as it bends and bends again. She feels her way along the walls and sometimes her hands rough along timbers and sometimes they push into the hollows and find the skulls recessed there.

She locates a room, foul with sweat, and it takes her many minutes to track its circumference. Her feet shuffle across blankets and furs and she guesses it to be a kind of bedroom.

From there she follows the tunnel again, counting her steps and maintaining a map in her mind, because her continued concentration is the only thing that keeps her from collapsing and tightening her body into a ball and giving up. She isn't sure what happened to her earlier, but she blames it on shock and stress and fear. A waking dream brought on by the flood of cortisol and norepinephrine in her system.

After another 203 steps, she enters a high, wide chamber. From the ceiling dangle long, thick roots. There are so many of them and they reach so low that it's like swimming through a kelp forest. Hanging from these roots, not all, but many of them, are objects that she fingers curiously. CDs. Tablets. Laptops. Smartphones. What might be the steering wheel of a boat? A silver dollar? With a hole punched through President Eisenhower's eye to accommodate the root's knot? The same thing has been done to hundreds of quarters.

She wends her way through the chamber until she comes across something heavy and solid that creaks the root with its weight. Her hands trace a buckle, a zipper. Her nails scritch the nylon. She knows then what she's found, but reaches up to ascertain her fear, and yes, there it is, the metal ball stippled with camera lenses. It's not just any backpack. It's a Titan pack.

All five of them, she soon discovers. The packs dangle from the roots like pupae. The death of her team felt like an abstract theory before. Now she feels burdened by the sudden weight of it all. She is the reason they came. She is the reason they're dead. She deserves to be down here with them, doomed to this place.

"Here there be dragons," she says to herself, and just then her hand nudges a switch, and the camera unit whirls to life with a rusty chirp. The darkness retreats as the chamber spins with a kalei- doscopic light. Map every inch of the world. That was their goal. But some places are better left undiscovered.

In the spinning light, she can see now that four tunnels reach outward from this chamber. The roots sway and the coins clink and the lights flash and she can only turn in circles when wondering which way to go. Until her very heart feels like it's spinning.

Then—coming from a low, oval entrance—a voice calls out to her. One she recognizes. A deep-throated rumble she heard often, speaking from the grainy reception of a satellite phone. Paul Meyer. From the earlier team. He had a black beard and thick forearms and previously worked for Outward Bound, leading troubled kids on wilderness adventures. He was from Ohio, she remembers. He liked horror movies. And rock climbing. And deep-dish pizza. His parents were in constant contact after he went missing, and she kept them updated as best she could. She emailed them a few days ago and told them she was assembling a new team. For rescue and recovery. "Don't give up hope," she wrote.

Now Paul is calling her name, over and over, "Michelle?" And he's not alone. Other voices weave in and out—is that Sammy? and Jane?—a summoning chorus, all crying for her to come. "Michelle?" they say. "This way, Michelle."

She goes to them. Following the tunnel into another chamber, this one a natural cave. Its floor is stone and black sand. At its entrance a lantern hangs from a hook and its light barely reaches the domed roof. She pulls the lantern down, surrounding herself with a hazy orange orb. A spring fountains out of the wall and splashes down a rough staircase of fallen rock and channels across the floor. The burble of water replaces the voices and she wonders a moment if that was the source all this time.

Along the floor and the walls and even the ceiling she notices roots. Some as thin as a finger. Others as broad as a thigh. They work through the dirt and through the stone, hundreds of them, thousands of them, interwoven. All veining outward from the same source. She follows them as they grow ever thicker, and now the lantern reveals their point of convergence.

It is watching her. A mass of roots that somehow appear knotted and woven and dirt-sculpted and stone-jeweled into the shape of a vast and terrible skull, but the skull of what she does not know. Something old. Something people would fall to their knees to worship. The roots that tumble down the walls and across the floor are its tongues or tentacles or veins. This is the base of the great tree she had encountered aboveground.

Every pulpit demands an offering, and this one has bodies upon it. Dozens of bodies. Both human and animal. Some are upside down. Some right-side up. Some sideways. With roots up their noses and down their throats and into their ears and eyes. Just as the cemetery outside featured boats new and old, so are the bodies here. She sees among them bones laced together with graying flaps of flesh. But she also smells the sweet stink of rot. Among the corpses she finds the faces of those she recognizes, their flesh preserved by the cold of the cave. Her team. She has finally found her team.

She doesn't realize she is screaming until the hand claps over her mouth.

Josh keeps calling her name, but Michelle doesn't seem to hear him. She drops the lantern and its glass shatters on the floor. She bites his hand hard enough to draw blood.

Even when she spins around and her eyes settle on him, even when he and Lester say, "It's okay—it's us," she keeps her distance. For every step they take toward her, she takes another back. She's streaked with grime and her eyes appear lidless, and she moves too wildly, swinging her arms and bending her knees too far with every retreating step. She doesn't breathe so much as gobble air. Words fight from her mouth when she says, "But is it you? Is it *really* you?"

They're going mad. All of them. This place is doing it.

Lester settles her down by holding his lantern toward a nearby body and saying, "Is it them? Your team?"

"It's them," she says, nodding sharply. "It's going to be us if we don't get the hell out of here."

"It already is us," Lester says, and they follow his gaze to Todd. He is naked. A fat root has wormed into his open mouth and down his throat. Another curls through his eye. Another goes into his ear. Others have entangled him elsewhere. Blood oozes off his body—and all the other bodies—and into the springwater that flushes its way downstream.

Her voice jitters when she says, "It's like a temple. It's like—" But she isn't sure what to say, because this isn't *like* anything. She wants to give it a name, but the only name it deserves is a scream.

Josh touches Todd—hesitantly at first. "No." His skin is cold. His body limp. "No." He searches for a pulse and can find none. "No." He pulls at the roots and thcy make a suckling sound when displaced. But he can't free his friend. "No, Todd. No, no." He hasn't opened himself up to sadness yet. There's only denial. And anger flaring on the other side of it.

"Let's go," Michelle says. "Let's just please go. We'll swim for it. It's a long way, but we can rest on the logs when we're tired and—"

She goes quiet as Lester lowers his lantern. His grip uncurls and it strikes the floor and tips over and the flame nearly dies.

"Lester?" Josh says, his hands still on Todd. "You okay?"

In response Lester lets out a wheezing sigh. Blood dribbles from his mouth, and he looks down at the prong that has suddenly appeared in his chest, the tip of an antler, shoved all the way through his back and out his breastbone, as though he were a sheath. When his body collapses, a man steps forward to take his place.

It's Josh. Or some version of him. The Josh who made it over the mountains. The Josh without scars hatching his skin. The Josh with a genuine smile brightening his face. Some figures approach, melting out of the darkness. His mother and father appear on either side of this happier, healthier version of himself and take his hands in theirs. Someone nudges between them, and they look down to chuckle at his sister, May. They all lean together affectionately. And then settle their eyes on him and wave him forward.

Maybe he would have gone. Maybe he would have joined them. If not for Michelle.

She scoops up the dropped lantern and leaps forward and swings it hard. Directly into the face of the other Josh. His face goes from a smile to a snarl and then transforms into a bear skull. A mask.

She swings the lantern again and the skull cracks and this time the lit kerosene splashes onto the man. For that is what he is. A man, not a phantom. A man who is screaming because his face is on fire. And when he swats at it, his hands catch on fire as well, and then his chest when he tries to extinguish them there.

Flames trail from the lantern like bright ribbons. She spins in a fast circle—and releases it. The lantern comets through the air with a sizzle. Then strikes the roots of the great tree. Maybe they twist and retract, but who can be sure in this indefinite light. Fire catches and a high-pitched keening follows. The sound comes from the witches.

Michelle grabs Josh's arm and drags him away and says, "Come on!" They kick their way into the stream, and the cave ceiling angles down sharply and they duck their heads and then drop to their knees to continue forward. "Where are we going?" he says and then understands as she forces her body flat and slides downstream and worms through a low hole in the cave wall. A band of moonlight is visible there, and he realizes it must be the same place they paused to drink earlier that day.

He drops down to follow her, but just then someone dives onto his leg and takes hold of it. A man with a long-jawed whale skull fitted over his own. Josh kicks at him until he is free. And then splashes and wriggles forward, into the short tunnel, the water surging all around him, a familiar feeling. His belt catches at one point, but he claws and scrambles his way out.

Michelle is on the other side, holding out her hand to him. But just as he grabs it, another snatches hold of his ankle. For a straining moment he is caught in the stream, still anchored to the underworld. He gives one last kick and slides free and pinwheels for a moment in the stream.

By the time he recovers and crawls onto the bank, he sees that Michelle has climbed onto the hillside over the tunnel. She kicks at a boulder, trying to dislodge it, straining down with her weight.

Below her—out of the darkness—the sharp white skull of the whale appears. Water froths around it. Then two arms appear and a torso, and just when the man is about to pull himself free, a few pebbles and a curtain of dirt come tumbling down onto him, followed by the boulder. It splinters the skull with a damp crunch and the shards of it are carried downstream, lost to the fragments of moonlight reflecting off the water's surface.

A fat moon hangs in the sky. Michelle has never liked the night, but she's always loved the moon. Because moonlight is different and special, almost always a surprise, silvering the world with a magical glow. It's something to pause and marvel at. "Look at the moon," people say, turning their faces upward. No one ever says that about the sun. Because it's our standard, our normal, our boring. Life is like sunlight. But dying is like moonlight. Maybe that explains her attraction to Josh. He is always on the brink of death, and that makes him unexpected and scarily beautiful. He is a kind of moon giving off his own special light.

Now she's joined him. She's never felt more vital, flooded with energy that brightens hidden pockets of herself she never knew existed. She is the one who saved them. She is the one guiding them through the woods now. She might have commissioned this expedition, but for the first time she truly feels in charge of it.

Josh's voice is high and pleading when he says, "Lester was the first friend to come see me in the hospital. After the crash. I remember waking up and seeing his face first. He was always there for me."

He seems to be talking more to himself than to her, but she still says, "I'm here for you now."

He can't seem to keep his balance as he blunders his hip into a stump and scrapes his forehead against a low-hanging branch. "My calf hurts," he says and she wants to say, Stop whining. He doesn't ask where they're going. And he doesn't thank Michelle or remark that she just killed a man or maybe more than one. They are beyond the reach of any map here, and also of rules.

"What did you see?" he says. "When you swung that lantern— what did you see?"

"I don't know," she says.

"What do you mean you don't know?"

"I mean—I don't trust the answer."

She smells smoke. Maybe it's roiling blackly through the tunnels now and leaking from hollowed trees as if through secret chimneys. Maybe the island was right to defend itself. Because mapping the world meant conquering it.

A flash of silver catches her eye and she pushes through a thorned and berried cluster of devil's club. "Found it," she says, uncovering a crab boat with its hull half-buried. Here begins the junkyard. Crashed planes and sunken ships dragged here to be claimed slowly by the elements.

"What did you see—in there?" he says again, and she says, "My team. I saw my team."

"The lost team?"

"Yes. I saw dead people. Okay?"

"That's not what I saw."

"Then I guess you haven't gone crazy like me." She doesn't want to think about it. She wants to focus on surviving. And the only way to do that is to find the aluminum canoe she spotted earlier. The velvety black air is broken up by silver shafts of moonlight that illuminate the wreckage.

"No," he says. "That's not what I mean. I saw my family."

She looks him hard in the eye. "What are you talking about?"

"And I saw myself."

She locates the canoe and asks for help as she sweeps the leaves and tears the vines off it and tips it over and dumps out the mildewed water and the two lacquer-peeled oars gathered at its bottom. "This way," she says and they hoist the canoe by the gunwales and portage toward the shore.

"What I saw kept changing. Like, the longer we were here, the worse it got. As if the island was figuring us out," he says. "Are they ghosts?"

She readjusts her grip. "Ghosts don't burn."

"Then what?"

"I don't know."

He can't stop talking, his words a babbling rush. "Whatever they are, it's like they're here in service of the place itself. Like that tree is one big witch. The island. The inlet. The surrounding forest. This entire fucking state." They push out of the trees and teeter down the shore.

"Does it matter what you call them?" she says, even as she recognizes his desire. He's acting like her. Wanting to put a pin in something. Label it. Stick it neatly in a drawer. But she's given herself over to the unknown.

They heave the canoe forward and it grumbles and scrapes across the rocks and then glides halfway onto the water. Michelle already has one leg inside it, and Josh is about to follow her when he hears a voice—a girl's voice—call out, "Wait."

The girl stands on the shore. The eyes of the deer skull are socketed black but he can feel her eyes watching him. "Don't leave." In her hand something glows. The satellite phone. "You forgot this."

Josh tries to concentrate on getting his legs to move. First one, then the other. He simply needs to climb in the canoe and shove off. But he can't. His mind feels as though it has shattered and out of the cracks have sprung roots that tunnel deep and hold him in place. He will never leave this place. It's where he belongs. And the girl is walking toward him now, reaching out her hand, offering the phone, and he can do nothing but say, "May? Is that you?"

Her voice deepens and her body fleshes out. "You're joking, right?" Todd says. "It's me, bro." He wears a Hawaiian shirt and cargo shorts and flip-flops.

"Where were you? I've been looking everywhere for you."

"Sorry, man. There's this great bar around the corner. Getting my happy hour on. First round's on me. Let's go?"

Josh ignores Michelle tugging at and pleading with him. The part of his brain that hasn't shut down remembers reading an article once about persistence hunting. Early humans would chase animals to death. Antelopes, gazelles, boars. Because we are uniquely suited for long-distance running, we can successfully chase down death or race away from it. That's what he's been doing all this time. Ever since the crash, he's never stopped running. But now he's ready to stop. He said as much back in Minnesota, right before he dove down that channel of water, the Devil's Kettle. "Remember?" Todd says. "You're the one who said it, bro. You're done."

"I'm done," Josh says.

"No more daring the nightmare. Time to kick back."

"I'm ready to rest."

"This is a good place for that. I know a good tree you can settle into the shade of for a nice long nap."

"As good a place as any."

"You said it, man."

The faces keep changing as the figure comes closer, and closer still, first Todd, now Lester, now his mother, now his father, finally his sister, and she grabs her ear and tugs hard and peels off her face and reveals the skull of a deer beneath it. Because Josh is screaming, he doesn't hear Michelle when she says, "Look at me! I'm right here, and right now I need you."

In the end, Michelle has to knock him out, curling her hands around the paddle and cracking its blade across the back of his head. She drags his body and flops it into the canoe and shoves off from shore. They're out on the water now, and she leans hard into every stroke, switching sides to fight the current that wants to push her back to the island.

She concentrates on her paddle. On the muscles burning in her shoulder. On finding her way through the many logs clogging the inlet. On the stars that will tell her where to go. She is concentrating so hard, she fails to see the girl tucked into the bow of the canoe. The girl wearing the deer mask. The girl with the sharpened antler clenched in her tiny hand.

Michelle is not sure how far away she is from the island—thirty yards, fifty, one hundred—when she hears a familiar two-toned whistle. She won't look back. Who knows what she'll find there. She imagines fires rising from below and embers fleeing the forest like bright autumn leaves. She imagines the witch tree uprooting itself and clambering after them with its long, dirt-clotted tentacles. She imagines hundreds of figures standing on the shore, watching her go, the island itself appearing like a humped black cairn.

Some things can't be captured by a photo. Some places don't align with maps. Some myths have yet to be discovered.

Acknowledgments

Thanks to the journals and magazines in which these stories originally appeared:

"The Cold Boy" (*Gulf Coast*), "Suspect Zero" (*Ellery Queen Mystery Magazine*), "The Dummy" (first published in *Cemetery Dance*; later collected in *XO Morpheus*, published by Penguin and edited by Kate Bernheimer), "Heart of a Bear" (*Orion*), "Dial Tone" (first published in the *Missouri Review*; later collected in *American Fantastic Tales*, published by the American Library Association and edited by Peter Straub), "The Mud Man" (the *Southern Review*), "Writs of Possession" (the *Virginia Quarterly Review*), "The Balloon" (first published in *Ploughshares*; later expanded and warped into a postapocalyptic novel, *The Dead Lands*), "Suicide Woods" (*McSweeney's*), and "The Uncharted" (*Full Bleed*).

Thanks to Larissa MacFarquhar for her reporting on the suicide culture of Japan—in "Last Call," published in the *New Yorker*—which inspired me to write the title story of this collection. And a special nod to Mary Shelley—the queen of darkness—for *Frankenstein* (especially chapters 11–16), without which I never would have written "Heart of a Bear."

Katherine Fausset. Steve Woodward, Jeff Shotts, Fiona McCrae, Marisa Atkinson, and the rest of the Graywolf crew. Holly Frederick and Noah Rosen and Britton Rizzio. Thanks to you all for the coaching and support.

And thanks, as always, to Lisa, for the love and friendship. Couldn't do it without you, Chief.

Benjamin Percy is the author of four novels—most recently, *The Dark Net* (Houghton Mifflin Harcourt, 2017)—as well as three books of short stories. His book of craft essays, *Thrill Me: Essays on Fiction*, is widely taught in creative writing classes.

His fiction and nonfiction have been published in *Esquire*, *GQ*, *Time*, *Men's Journal*, *Outside*, the *Wall Street Journal*, *Tin House*, *Ploughshares*, *Glimmer Train*, *McSweeney's*, and the *Paris Review*. His honors include an NEA Fellowship, the Whiting Award, the Plimpton Prize, two Pushcart Prizes, and inclusion in *Best American Short Stories* and *Best American Comics*.

He broke into comics in 2014 with a Batman story in Detective Comics, and has gone on to write celebrated runs on Wolverine, Nightwing, Green Arrow, Teen Titans, and James Bond for Marvel, DC, and Dynamite.

The text of *Suicide Woods* is set in Utopia Std. Book design by Ann Sudmeier. Composition by Bookmobile Design & Digital Publisher Services, Minneapolis, Minnesota. Manufactured by Versa Press on acid-free, 30 percent postconsumer wastepaper.